GUILTY PLEASURES

A LOVE TRIANGLE

T.L. BLAKELY

Guilty Pleasures

Copyright © 2017 by T.L. Blakely

Published by Mz. Lady P Presents

www.mzladypresents.com

SYNOPSIS

Being best friends since kindergarten, Shay and Marie were inseparable. Everyone ain't your friend was the motto they lived by and were prepared to die by, but when the tables turn and jealousy comes into play, Marie does something she will eventually regret. Not knowing what to do in this situation, will she learn that the self-made motto was all too real, even in their "forever" friendship?

Jerome Hamilton is a name that is very popular throughout Antioch High School. Jerome is the star basketball player with phenomenal skills on and off the court. Growing up his father was in the army, so he rarely got that father/son love he craved, and he was never shown how to treat a woman with respect. The person he thought he could put his trust and love in showed him everything that glitters ain't gold. With deceit, disloyalty, and stories that just don't add up, will Jerome be able to ever truly trust again, will he lose his career?

Find out in T.L. Blakely's debut novel Guilty Pleasures: A Love Triangle

ACKNOWLEDGMENTS

First, and foremost, I would like to thank my heavenly Father. Without you, none of this would've been possible. Thank you for blessing me with an awesome gift. I am so glad that I found my gift to share with the world.

I thank my friends and family for supporting me while writing this book. I thank you guys for helping me with ideas when I couldn't think of anything. I would like to thank my son Albert for showing me that smile when I was feeling down. Thank you for being mommy's motivation every day. I would like to thank my sister Precious for always reading the book when I felt it wasn't good enough. Thanks for always telling me to never give on writing. I would also like to thank my best friend/ my love Shawn for always believing in me. Thank you for always being by my side when I felt like giving up. No matter what you have always been there through thick and thin. I would also like to thank a few of my author friends Ni'Andra, November, Yatta Rose, Miyah, Kyeate, Kandie Marie, Shay Renee, Autumn Rose, Brittany Williams, Tabitha Sharpe, Quardeay, and Elijah Foreman. I appreciate you guys always giving me advice when I needed it. Thanks for always test reading the book when I felt like it wasn't good enough. You guys are all my inspiration. I love you.

Lakeitha Chatman, thank you for being the best test reader. I appreciate you always taking the time out to read my books. Love you, girl.

I want to thank my publisher, Mz. Lady P for giving me the best opportunity in my life. I'm so glad you saw potential in me to add me to your team. To my lovely pen sisters, thank you for helping me when I needed it and putting up with my crybaby ass. I love y'all. #MLPP

Writing books isn't just something I was blessed with. God created the gift within me.

-Author T.L. Blakely

SHAY

"Prom tickets! Come get your prom tickets!"

I couldn't believe this was my senior of 2010. Prom was right around the corner. I still didn't have a date. All these dudes around the school and nobody even asked me. I guess I was too damn skinny for them. All the thick or fat girls had dates but me. I hated being the skinny girl at times. I was a late bloomer, so I barely had breasts or an ass. I had my eyes on this one dude name Jerome, but my best friend Marie was going to prom with him. How could she get a date before me? This was so unfair.

I'm sorry for being rude. My name is La'Shayla Nicole Barnes. I'm a senior at Antioch High School. Yes, home of the Bears as the principal would say every morning before the announcements. I was the person that was smart but cool with everyone in the school. Being that I was very smart, I'll be graduating with honors in a few weeks, which was very exciting. Being the first high school graduate in my family was a big accomplishment. I just wanted to make my family proud.

I was the oldest of three children. I was the only child with a different dad though. I hated it because I felt out of place. My stepdad treated me with respect, but I knew deep down that I wasn't his. I

1

knew who my biological father was, but I guess my mother didn't want to tell me the truth. It was very hurtful, but I just left the situation alone. I didn't want to be the reason for drama in the house, so I promised myself when I turned eighteen I would reconnect with my biological father. I just wanted to have that father-daughter relationship I never had growing up.

"La'Shayla?"

"What girl, why you are running down the hallway like that? "

"I may have you a prom date."

"Who is it? He better not be ugly either bitch."

"Chauncey Jones"

"Bitch, he is not that cute. You tryna set me up for the kill."

"Girl, I'm just trying to help you out. I'm tired of your skinny ass complaining to me about it."

"Fine, I'll go with him then."

"Alright, I'll give him your number. I'll see you after class."

I was so pissed at Marie. She always did this shit. If I didn't have a date, she would hook me with someone ugly as hell. I mean Chauncey wasn't ugly. His damn teeth were just so damn big. It reminded of a damn horse. Every time he would open his mouth, all you can see was them big ass teeth. What made it worse was that he had braces. I just couldn't believe her. I'm thankful for her helping me find a date, but damn, why him out of all people.

Walking to dance class, I received a text from an unknown number. *Who the hell is this?* I thought.

Unknown: Hey, beautiful. I'm so glad you decided to go to prom with me.

Me: No problem. I want to wear lavender and black. We can meet after school to talk about it.

Unknown: Okay, beautiful. See you then.

Before walking into class, I saw Jerome going to gym class. He was so fine. I know my best friend was dating him, but he would eventually be mine. Just watching him from afar gave me butterflies. He eventually looked my way and waved. I began to get hot, so I decided to go inside my class. Dance was my favorite class. I had practice during the day because I was on the majorette team. I loved dancing. It was my escape to my troubles in my life. I sat down reading a book called *A Savage and His Lady* by Kyeate. Reading was another thing I loved doing as well. It helped me relax and soothed my mind.

"Shay, did you find a date to the prom? Alexis asked.

"Yes, I'm going with Chauncey Jones."

"The rich boy, Chauncey Jones?"

"Unfortunately, yes."

"Well girl, he's got money. You probably won't have to pay for anything."

"Alexis, girl, I don't need his money. I have my own money. Why you think I have a job. I don't have a silver spoon in my mouth like you do. Now if you can please move so that I can stretch."

Alexis seriously got on my nerves. The bitch was nosy as hell. Like why hoes couldn't mind they business. That's exactly why I kept to myself at school. I didn't like drama, and I wasn't about to deal with any when school was almost over. I could see her talking to the other dancers about me, but I didn't care. The bitch was so scary anyway.

"Come on, girls. It's time to rehearse for the dance show."

I was excited about the dance show this weekend. I had two solos that I would be performing. The dance coach from MTSU would be coming to watch me perform. I applied to MTSU some months ago and was accepted on a full dance scholarship. I just hoped my parents allowed me to go. My parents were very overprotective. I could barely do anything with them asking me so questions. I wasn't even prepared about telling them I had a prom date either. That one conversation needed to be avoided for now.

Class was finally over. I was headed to lunch when someone grabbed my arm. Jerome was standing there with that big ass smile. Looking him up and down, I tried to avoid eye contact. This boy was making my mind go into a place with naughty thoughts. I needed to get away from before anyone saw me with him. One thing to avoid is an argument with my best friend after school.

"Hey, Shay, where you about to go?"

"I'm headed to lunch."

"Can I join you?"

"I'm heading to Sonic."

"Well, let me drive. I want you to reserve your gas, love."

"Jerome, where is Marie? Are you going to ask if she wants to come along?

"Naw, she's probably going to finish up some homework."

"Alright, let's go."

I felt so bad about going to lunch with Jerome without Marie. It felt so weird without her with us. He offered so I couldn't resist it. I really hoped no one would see us. The last thing I needed was someone running back telling her what happened. Marie was my best friend, and I didn't want to hurt her. I said a small prayer hoping God answered my prayer.

We had arrived at Sonic within fifteen minutes. I was starving. I decided to order two double cheeseburgers, onion rings, and large root beer. Jerome had ordered two chilidogs with some tater tots and a large coke. We both were quiet until we were half done with our food. He kept staring at me, which made me very uncomfortable. I looked away to avoid him looking at me.

"So, Shay, are you going to prom? You got a date yet?"

"Yes, I have a date. I'm going with Chauncey Jones."

"You're going to the prom with horse teeth?" he said while laughing hysterically.

"Hell, he was the last option. Marie hooked it up."

"He is a good guy. So just enjoy the prom."

"Well, we should be getting back."

As we were heading back to the school, Jerome received a call from Marie. He hit declined to avoid an argument with her. I knew it would probably be some drama when we arrived back at school. I just hoped Marie didn't blow the situation out of proportion. Her attitude was real rude when it came to communication. She couldn't really communicate without yelling or screaming at someone.

Finally, we arrived at the school in Marie was standing in the front waiting. I rolled my eyes because I knew what was about to occur. Before Jerome got out, he handed me his number to text him. I just took it in stuck it in my bag. I may not ever use this number, but I kept it for emergency purposes. I stepped out the car. Walking towards the school, Marie came running towards me crying. She could be so dramatic at times. I really wasn't about to argue in front of these people either, so I walked passed her without saying anything? Certain things just didn't need a reaction, so I ignored her ass. We just went to lunch that's it.

"Shay, why did you go to lunch with my boyfriend?"

"First of all, Marie, he asked to join me. I don't want your man. He is all yours. Now if you can move so that I can go to class."

"Well bitch, if I catch you around him again you gone wish it never happened."

"Marie, your threats don't scare me. You don't even like Jerome like that. You better shut up before I tell your secret."

"Whatever. Remember what I said."

Leaving her there looking confused, I went to my next class. I didn't have time for her nonsense today. I so used to our arguments though. We did this all the time since preschool days. She will eventually apologize when she realized she was wrong. I loved her, but she knew not to go there with me.

MARIE

"*M*arie?"

"What, Alexis?"

"Girl, I saw Shay leaving the school with Jerome. I just wanted to let you know since that's your best friend in all."

"Do you know where they went off to? I think they went to Sonic. Well, thanks, girl. See ya later."

After that news, I was so hurt. How could my best friend of fifteen years betray me like this? I ran to the bathroom and hid in one of the stalls. That was my boyfriend, and she was going off to lunch with him. Why didn't they ask could I go? This was so beyond sneaky. I couldn't wait till they got back. I was going to literally show my ass. Never mind, scratch that. It was too close to graduation and prom. I couldn't afford to get in trouble right now. I was going to keep calm.

Getting up out the stall, I cleaned my face up. I probably was over-reacting anyway. I knew Shay wouldn't do anything to hurt me anyway. Alexis didn't like Shay because she was co-captain of the dance team, so I couldn't really trust her. I had found out from the source on what happened anyway. Shay was just going with him because he probably asked. I did have to catch up on some homework from math class anyway. My math was the only class I was struggling in. That was the only class that would determine if I graduate or not. I had to make sure I did everything I could do to pass this class.

Unlike Shay, I wasn't as smart as she was. I barely passed my classes. I always made B's and C's maybe some D's if I didn't try my best. See, I was the older of two children. It was me, Marie Renee Jones and my brother Malachi Redmond Jones. Yes, we were both twins. We lived with my dad and grandmother. My mother had left us at five years old because she was having an affair with her boss at work. My dad found out about it and was very hurt. He wanted a divorce from her. Since then our mother has not been a part of our lives. Every time we tried to reach out to her, her husband would always say she was busy, so we just quit trying. I was really hoping she received my letter that I sent her about my graduation and prom. I really want her to be a part of it.

Leaving out the bathroom, I decided to go to the library and read my book on Kindle by November titled *The Air My King Breathes*. I just needed to get my mind off things. I decided to text Jerome to see what was up. I didn't need to be acting all insecure either. We had only been together for almost five months, so I shouldn't be tripping over anything. I mean Jerome never gave me reasons to doubt him anyway.

Me: Baby, where you at?

Baby Love: I'm at Sonic with Shay.

Me: Why didn't you ask me to come, baby? That really hurts.

Baby: Babe, you know you had work to finish. I didn't want to distract you from that all. Your classwork comes before anything. You know that class determines if you graduate or not.

Me: Yes, you're right. Can we go tonight?

Baby: No, sorry I have basketball practice tonight. We can reschedule for the weekend.

Me: Okay, baby. See you when you get back.

Baby: See you then.

I was so upset because Jerome didn't want to go to dinner tonight. I was off from TJ MAX today, and I wanted to do something fun. I guess I needed to study for these upcoming exams. I left the library and waited outside till they came. I was going to confront Shay on this bullshit. Just because my man asked her to do something didn't mean she had to. After today, she will know not to fuck with me. I tried to calm down but couldn't do that. My anger issues were kicking in.

They pulled up in I saw Shay walking towards me. I just wanted to slap the smug look on her face. The bitch got life fucked up if she thought she was taking my man from me. I would beat his ass and her ass. I needed to calm down before I did anything that I would regret. It was some weeks before prom and graduation. I counted to ten before I spazzed out. I did this when I knew my anger was getting out of control. I ran towards her crying, so I confront the disrespectful bitch.

"Shay, why did you go to lunch with my boyfriend?"

"First of all, Marie, he asked to join me. I don't want your man. He is all yours. Now if you can move so that I can go to class."

"Well bitch, if I catch you around him again, you gone wish it never happened."

"Marie, your threats don't scare me. You don't even like Jerome like that. You better shut up before I tell your secret."

"Whatever. Remember what I said."

As she walked off, I ran towards Jerome. I was so pissed off that I started punching him. I couldn't resist it. How could he be so disrespectful? I was hurting, and him taking her to lunch wasn't cool at all. I had a lot of issues going on, and he was the only one to take it out on. I just hope I wouldn't regret this.

"Stop fucking putting your hands on me, Marie. I'm so sick of your ass. Every time you get in your feelings, you want to fight. I'm sick of this bullshit."

"Jerome, I'm sorry you know I'm falling for you. I get so jealous at times. Please forgive me."

"Alright, man. I'll call you after practice."

"Okay."

Jerome walked away, and I felt bad about what I did. I always let my anger get the best of me. It was something I needed to work on. The things that were going in my life were taking a toll on me. I tried to pray on the things, but I sometimes felt that prayer didn't work. Until then I'll watch Shay and Jerome closely.

JEROME

"*J*erome, nigga, did I just see you get out the car with Shay?" my best friend, Calvin said.

"Yes, I did. We only went to lunch, my nigga."

"I know you, nigga. You can't just go out with a girl and not give her the D, bro."

"Bruh, I didn't have sex with her ass. Get the fuck out my face with all that bullshit. "

"Damn nigga, get out ya feelings."

"You mind ya damn business. "

I was irritated as hell with Calvin ass. He was questioning me like he was my daddy or something. Calvin and Marie both had me pissed now. I couldn't get over Marie putting her hands on me. I was really getting tired of her bullshit. Her anger issues were getting the best of her. She had too many family issues she was dealing with. I always offered her counseling at my church, but she refused to go. I thought if she got counseling she would be able to talk about her issues in life. If she wanted to change her life, she would have to want it. My mama always said you couldn't change someone who doesn't want to change.

I'm Jerome Nathan Hamilton. I am the youngest of the family. I have a brother name, Braxton Neil Hamilton. Braxton is not my real biological brother. My parents adopted him into the family because my mother's sister was on drugs at the time. We barely got along due to him wanting to be a thug and sell drugs. He was five years older than I was, so he was barely home. My parents let him stay in the house knowing he was selling drugs, which pissed me off. They appreciated him bringing the money in. I just focused on graduating and getting accepted to MTSU for basketball.

My parents were not on the best of terms right now. They were currently filing for a divorce. My dad was no longer happy with my mother. I didn't know the reason why they suddenly wanted a divorce. This was my last year of high school, and this was happening to me. I felt so hurt after hearing this news. My mother, Diane Hamilton, worked at Vanderbilt Medical Center. She was the charge nurse of the pediatric department. My mom was very beautiful. She stood at 5'10 with mocha brown skin. She was mixed with Somalian and black. I loved my mom, and I hated to see her hurting. As far as my dad, David Hamilton, he was in the army. He had been in the army since he graduated high school. Growing up, he was barely even home, which I hated. To keep me happy he always made sure I had the latest shoes and latest fashions to rock. I didn't care for all the materialistic things. I just wanted to have a closer relationship with my father.

Snapping me out of my thoughts, I received a text from Shay telling me to lock her number in. I smiled so hard looking at that text. This feeling for Shay was a feeling I never felt before. Her smile was intoxicating. Her personality was to die for. She was so calm, cool, and collected. She stood at 5'5 probably 130 pounds. She wore her hair in its natural state. Her body shape was very petite with a little booty to match. The skin tone she had was a mocha type brown. Looking like an Ethiopian queen, she was very attractive to me. I knew I was in a relationship, but I wanted to get to know Shay a little better. I sent her a text to see if I could take her out.

Me: Would you like to go out Friday night after the game?

Future Bae: That would be cool. Why aren't you taking Marie out?

Me: I want to take you out. I want to know La'Shayla better.
Future Bae: Alright, just let me know where and what time.
Me: Alright, I will beautiful.

In the locker room, I saw the new water boy, Malachi. I knew he was Marie's twin, but we really didn't talk when I came to the house. Something was off about him, but I couldn't put my finger on it. Most people called him gay, but I didn't because I wanted to know from the source. I never judged someone before I knew the actual person. I treated everyone with respect.

Headed to the gym, I was ready to get this practice over with. Friday would be the last game of the season until the championship. This game will determine if I get my scholarship to MTSU. I was praying God would bless me with this opportunity. I know my relationship with him wasn't like it needed to be, but I just hope it works out. My dream growing up was to go to the NBA. I wanted to play with my favorite basketball team, the Los Angeles Lakers. Kobe Bryant is who inspired me. I watched everything he did on the court. So, Friday I will have to play my heart out.

* * *

TWO HOURS later practice was finally over. I went to the dance room to see if Shay was in there. I saw her practicing looking all beautiful. Just looking at her gave me sudden butterflies. I just prayed someday that she would eventually be mine. She glanced over at me and smiled. Practice must've been over because everyone was leaving off the dance floor. I waited until she came out to let her know I was leaving. I didn't want her to walk to her car by herself.

She finally came out the dance room. I could she looked frustrated a little bit. I wondered if the performance Friday was stressing her out. I think taking her out on an ice cream date would make her feel better.

"You alright, beautiful?"

"No, not really, one of my solos is getting taken out of the dance show Friday. "

12

"Well, you're already performing one solo, right?"

"Yes."

"You will still have a chance to kill that one solo. Just stay positive sweetheart."

"Alright, thank you."

"Would you like to get something to eat before heading home? We could to Pizza Hut or something. I'll pay for it. "

"Why do you want to spend so much time with me? You and Marie are still together, Jerome. I don't feel comfortable sneaking around behind her back.

"Look, baby, don't worry about her. This is between us, alright?

"Alright, we can go."

I walked over to her door and opened it. I was trying to show her that I wanted her. Shay was not like the girls in school. She was very different from them. Her head was on straight. I wanted to give all my time to her. It was wrong for me to do this behind Marie back, but I didn't care. She was the one who was pushing me away. She always takes her issues out on me, which I was tired of. At some point in time, I would have to break it off with Marie. On the other hand, maybe I could have both at the same time. No, that's not right. Karma is a real bitch these days. I was just going to let this flow out because I wasn't trying to hurt anyone.

We both arrived at Pizza Hut on Nolensville Road. This was my favorite to come to. It was literally right around the corner from my house. Looking over at her, I noticed she was still beautiful but frustrated. The way her lips poked out, I just wanted to kiss them. The guilt started to come over me when I missed a call from Marie. Thinking about it made me want to cancel it. I do shouldn't this. It's wrong on so many levels. I sent Marie a text to let her know I'll call her later.

Me: I'll call you later.

Marie: Why can't you call me now? What are you doing?

Me: Damn, girl. I just got out of practice. I got to go home and shower in stuff.

Marie: Alright. Ttyl.

As soon as I ended the text with Marie, I saw Shay giving me an evil look. I knew she wasn't feeling this. I shouldn't put her in this position. I decided to just take her back to her car. Shay and Marie had been best friends for too long for me to end it over this. I couldn't deny the way I felt about Shay though. I would just have to be patient until the day comes for her to become mine.

SHAY

$\mathcal{I}$ was so glad Jerome was taking me back to the car. I wasn't feeling this going behind back Marie to hang with her boyfriend. I was not the type of girl to mess with a dude who had a girlfriend. Stuff like that didn't satisfy me in any way. Jerome should just work things out with Marie. Whatever issues they were having, they needed to communicate about it. Communication is key in every relationship.

I finally arrived back to my car. I just wanted to go home and sleep this frustration off. I was still upset about one of my solos being taken out of the show. I didn't know what was up with that. I slick think Alexis' hating ass had something to do with it. She was so mad at the fact I became co-captain of the majorette team. She had a bad attitude problem and she couldn't communicate with other dance members very well. That's basically why I was chosen to be captain.

My phone started vibrating. It was Chauncey calling me. I wonder what he wanted this time of night. I was thinking about what if I did give Chauncey a chance. It wouldn't hurt to give him one. I wonder if he was doing anything tonight. He was calling for a third time, and I finally answered.

"Hey, Chauncey."

"What's up, beautiful?"

"Nothing about to go home. I'm hungry really. I haven't eaten anything."

"Well, you can pull up to my crib. My parents are cooking some fish and spaghetti tonight."

"They wouldn't mind me coming over?"

"Naw, sweetheart. They want to meet you anyway since I'm taking you to prom."

"What's the address?"

"I live in Summerfield."

"I know where that is. Just send me the address."

"See you in a few."

I was headed to Chauncey's house when my mama texted me. She basically was telling me I needed to be home in twenty minutes. I hated that I had an early curfew. She treated me like I was a child. I was eighteen years old now. This overprotective mess was too much for me. I can't wait to graduate so that I live on campus. Living in that house was pure hell. I wanted peace in my life. I thought about going to stay with my grandmother, but I knew she would be hesitant on that. I was going to see Chauncey regardless of her texting me that bullshit.

I finally pulled up to Chauncey house. I wasn't going in because I needed to be getting home. I didn't want my mother having a reason to argue tonight. He finally came outside looking fine as hell even with those big ass horse teeth. He was rocking a gray Nike jumpsuit with some Nike flip-flops on. Chauncey was brown skin and tall as hell. He wore a tapered fade and had a full-grown beard to just be eighteen years old. He was Ethiopian and black. His family was very wealthy. The money didn't impress me though because I made my own money. Being that he hung around a lot of thugs and drug dealers, he was still smart. I didn't know why he hung around that crowd, but I knew it wasn't a good look for him. I just hope he was very careful hanging around them.

"Hey, La'Shayla."

"Why you say it like that."

"Just to make you smile, love."

"Well, I can't stay long. My mother is a little strict. "

"Trust me you don't got to explain anything to be about parents being strict. My parents are strict as well. "

"Well, I want you to at least meet my parents. They won't bite, Shay. "

"Alright, I'll come in for a few minutes."

Once we got in the house, my mama started to call me. I pressed ignore to avoid any drama with her. I wish she would understand that I'm not a child anymore. I really didn't want to show Chauncey that something wrong with me. He would feel like I'm rude if I just leave the house without meeting his parents. I would just go to the bathroom to speak to my mother. That way I could avoid any drama at these people house.

"Chauncey, where is the bathroom?"

"It's down the hall to the left."

"Alright, thank you."

I got to the bathroom and answered on the third ring. I was hesitant at first, but I went on and answered it.

"La'Shayla, get your black ass home right now. You're not grown. I told you to be home twenty minutes ago. Where the fuck you at?"

"I'm at my friend's house. I'm not doing anything wrong at all. This is the person I'm going to prom with. Why are you acting this way?"

"Bitch, don't question me. I'm the parent. I don't have to explain shit to you. Bring your ass home now!"

"Okay, mama."

I literally had tears in my eyes coming out the bathroom. I seriously hated my life. How can a mother treat her first child this way? I felt like she still had a grudge against my dad. I didn't have anything to do with what happened between them. I felt like I didn't deserve to be here. I wanted to move back home with my grandmother. I wondered if my grandmother knew what her daughter was doing to me. I will be calling her tonight. I walked out the bathroom and Chauncey and his parents were staring at me. I knew they wanted to ask questions but didn't bother asking.

"Chauncey I'm going home. My mama is very upset about me not coming straight home. I'm sorry."

"It's okay, beautiful. These are my parents. We all heard you crying. Is it safe for you to go home tonight?"

"Yes, I'll be fine."

"Call me if you need me to come gets you, love."

"Alright. Nice meeting you guys."

I ran to my car and cried uncontrollably. I didn't want to go home. I hated it there. My mother treated me like shit for no reason. I seriously hated my life. That household was pure misery. I couldn't wait to graduate in a couple of weeks. I would work every day until I go to college. She got life fucked up if she thought she would keep treating me this way. I would have to stand my ground tonight. I was being too nice. Mother or not, I deserved respect. I was going to get it tonight.

* * *

PULLING UP TO MY HOUSE, there were police cars everywhere. I didn't know what was going on. I got out the car to ask my siblings what happened.

"What's going on?"

"Mama and daddy got into it. Mama pulled a knife on daddy. I guess daddy was cheating on her with another woman. That's why she kept calling you, Shay. We don't want to go to foster care."

"Look, no one is going anywhere. Stop crying. I will make sure you guys are taking care of. Stay right here."

I went towards the house, but my mama was in the police car crying. I really didn't give two fucks about her ass right now. Her miserable ass deserved it. Maybe if she didn't nag him so much, she wouldn't be in this situation. I saw my stepdad in the ambulance with a bloody towel on his arm. I felt sorry for him. Now, I would have to call my grandmother to come stay with us for a while until this situation got better.

I got my siblings in we went back into the house. They were all tired from tonight's events, so I put them to bed. I was the oldest, so it was my responsibility to take care of them. I could tell they were hurting because mama was not staying here tonight. I wonder where she would go. It was the least of my worries right now. Her actions got her in this position anyway. My mother suffered from a bipolar disorder. Basically, it was a disorder associated with different mood swings ranging from depressive lows to manic highs. She had been that way since her dad passed away from prostate cancer. Mom and her dad were very close. She was a daddy's girl.

My mom was very smart and talented. She could sing her ass off. My mama was 5'10 with a big booty. She was brown skin woman. My mama worked only on weekends as a certified nursing assistant. She worked in the department with the children who suffered from cancer. Her passion was to always with children. She had just recently got a promotion to become the supervisor of that department. This disorder had become a problem in their marriage. My stepdad tried so many times to get her help, but she would never go. They even tried counseling, but that didn't work either. I prayed every day for them. Hopefully, their marriage gets better.

I checked on the kids again to make sure they were straight. They were sleeping so peacefully. I loved my siblings. I hated that I would be leaving them soon. I would have to promise them that I would be home every weekend to visit them. I got settled and fixed me something to eat since I didn't eat at Chauncey's house. I checked my phone with three calls from Chauncey, one text message from Marie, and two messages from Jerome. I smiled that Chauncey had called. I guess he was just making sure I was alright after I left. He was really a sweet guy. I picked my phone up to call him back.

"Hey beautiful, you alright? You had me worried sick."

"Yes, I'm alright. I've just got some family issues going on right now. I'm just up eating."

"What you are eating, love?"

"Just a bologna sandwich."

"Well, I'll see you at school tomorrow. Goodnight, beautiful."

"Night."

I went to my room smiling so hard. Chauncey had me feeling some type of way. What I said about him was very mean. I was slowly becoming attracted to him. I already knew he felt the same way about me as well. I couldn't wait to see him tomorrow.

MARIE

I was so bored tonight. All I was doing was studying for this stupid math exam. I hated studying, especially for math. I prayed I passed this shit because I hated high school. My dad tried to help me as much as he could, but I still struggled with it. I wanted to call Jerome, but he was still at basketball practice. I decided to ask my brother could he help me. I really didn't know if he was home yet. He was the water boy for the basketball team. The last person I could ask was my grandmother.

I walked towards her room. Her door was cracked, but she wasn't in there. I wondered if she was in the living room watching Lifetime. My grandmother, Leona, was a great woman. She raised my brother and me when my mother left us for that Uncle Tom. I couldn't believe my mother would do that to my dad. He sacrificed so much for her. I noticed my grandmother was sleep. I heard my phone vibrating in my room. I hope it was my baby. I needed to see him.

"Hello."

"Hey babe, what are you doing?"

"Nothing, trying to study but this math work is hard. Can you come help me please?"

"Yes, I'm on the way. Is your grandmother home?'

"She is sleep, but you can still come."

"Be there in a few."

I was glad my baby was on the way. I needed some dick to relieve this stress. I just hope I didn't get caught while doing it. I was really playing with fire knowing that my grandmother was asleep in the living room. If I get caught, Lord knows I wouldn't hear the end of this. I went to the living to make sure she was still asleep. Thank God, she was. I rushed to the shower to wash up a little bit. I wanted to be fresh before Jerome pulled up. I was taught to always be fresh before getting some dick, and I never questioned it.

I jumped in the shower. I was very into being hygienic, so I had to smell good around him. I took at least three showers a day. My dad would be pissed when he saw the water bill. That's how much I washed my ass. Being OCD had something to do with that as well. I always made sure the house was clean. Something about the smell of Pine Sol and bleach made me happy. Just being in a clean house always made things easier. You wouldn't have to worry about company coming over, and the house was dirty.

Since my grandmother was getting older, it was best that I picked up extra chores, so she could rest and watch her television shows. My grandmother was a nurse at Centennial Hospital. She was now a retired nurse who worked there for forty plus years. She inspired me in so many ways because I wanted to be a nurse at St. Jude Hospital in Memphis. After high school, I planned on going through the TCAT program so that I can become a nurse within eighteen months. I didn't want to go to a university, because that was just waste money I think. Plus, my daddy wasn't going for me living on campus away from him. With him not having my mother around, he needed all of us for moral support. I wish he could start dating soon because his lonely ass was getting on my damn nerves.

I heard Jerome loud ass music coming from around the corner. I hope he didn't wake my grandmother up. She hated when he pulled up with that loud ass devil music he is playing, as she would say. My grandmother hated any music other than gospel. She would always say that music was corrupting our minds. I loved trap music I just didn't listen to around her ass.

I went to the door to open it, so he could just come right on in. I try to avoid any loud noise because my grandmother was a light sleeper. If a damn pen dropped, she would probably hear it. Hopefully, she wouldn't wake up while we were making love because I didn't need her spoiling the mood.

Jerome walked in looking fine as hell. His Polo cologne always smelled so good. I began to kiss him passionately. He placed my hand on his bulge in his gray Nike sweatpants. For him to be this young, he sure was packing down there. I walked him to my bedroom so that we could have some privacy. I couldn't wait to get my wet mouth on his long pole. I went to my dresser to grab my Jolly Ranchers off the dresser. I loved having candy in my mouth while sucking dick. I learned this trick from my cousin when I was like fourteen years old. So since then I only did this trick on niggas that were special to me. I unwrapped the candy and began to rub his shaft up and down so that he could at least get a bit harder. I wasn't a pro at deep throating, but hell, I was going to try tonight.

Placing the Jolly Rancher in my mouth, I then grabbed his dick, placing it into my wet mouth. I begin to suck the tip until his dick grew a bit more. I wanted to take this nigga soul from his body tonight. When it came to sucking dick, I wanted niggas to know my head game was strong. Peeking at Jerome, I could see he loved every minute of this.

"Damn, Marie!"

"You like that, baby?"

"Hell yea, don't stop. I want you to swallow this all nut in ya mouth."

"You know damn well I don't swallow. Don't fucking play, nigga."

Jerome got up and threw my ass on the bed after I said that. Looking at him while lying down made me even wetter. His long pole looked even bigger laying there. I wish he could come on and put it in, damn. He was taking his lil time just rubbing my juice box with his tip. I was starting to get irritated because he was just playing when I wanted to get some dick.

"Jerome, hurry the fuck up, damn!"

"Baby, calm down. I don't want to just fuck you. I want to make love."

"Boy, you don't know how to make no damn love. Just give me some dick and quit playing with my damn emotions."

Jerome placed his tip inside, and I nearly woke my damn grandmother up. Like this nigga was literally going to have me handicapped. He really thought he was he was gone put them nine inches all in my guts, he thought wrong. This lil pussy of mine wouldn't be able to handle this shit. He began to push his dick inside inch by inch. I began to get even wetter because he was hitting my spot constantly. I rotated my hips to match his rhythm. I loved every minute of this shit. My eyes began to roll to the back of my head.

"Ohhhh, Jerome, right there baby. That shit feels good."

"You like that shit don't you, baby?"

"Yes, I really do. Go deeper! Go deeper! Goooo deeper!"

He picked up the pace, and I couldn't hold my screams any longer. I screamed like a big ten-pound baby was coming out of me. I felt my body about to climax, and I came all over his long pole. He flipped me over, so I positioned myself on all fours. He rammed his dick inside. Arching my back deep, I felt every inch of his dick in my stomach. He began to pound my pussy so good. I couldn't scream, so I put my face insides the pillow to avoid waking my grandmother. If she knew what I was doing, I would be six feet under.

"Jerome, I'm about to cum. Baby, cum with me."

"Alright baby, I'm cumming, I'm cumming.

He finally nutted inside me, and I remembered that I forgot to use a condom. Shit, I was ovulating today too. The chances of me being pregnant in a couple of weeks scared the shit out of me. How could I be so damn stupid? But hell, that dick was good as fuck.

"Marie! Marie! Marie!"

My grandmother was coming towards my room, and I couldn't even hide Jerome anywhere. I had to think of something quick.

However, I couldn't since his as was damn near sleep on my bed. He was about to get my ass caught. I couldn't let my grandmother catch me with him naked in my bed. I wouldn't hear the last of this.

"Jerome, get up. My grandmother is up. Hide in the closet."

"Alright."

BOOM!

"What the fuck is your fast ass doing in here with this boy naked?"

"Um, granny we were playing, well wrestling."

"Girl, don't play dumb with me. Your ass was having sex. Wait till I tell your daddy this. Little boy, put ya dick up and get the fuck out my house."

"Granny, I'm sorry. I'm sorry."

"Shut up. We will talk later. "

Jerome walked out the room mad as hell. I didn't even get a kiss goodbye. My grandmother was pissed as well. I could hear her talking to my dad on the phone. He probably was going to beat my black ass. The fucked-up part about is we didn't use a condom. How stupid could I be? I would just have to live up to this mistake I just made.

I went to the bathroom to clean myself up. I felt so bad about upsetting my grandmother. I knew my dad would be pissed as well. My dad was going to be within the next thirty minutes. I knew he was going to lecture the hell out of me too. My dad did not tolerate having sex before marriage. He always told me never to give my promise diamond to anybody. He said that my body was my temple and only my husband was able to know about it. I wasn't really into that religious thing. I mean I went to church, but I just wasn't into all that.

Malachi had come into my room trying to be nosy. I really didn't want to hear whatever he had to say. He tended to always try to take sides with my grandmother. We weren't that close these days because Malachi had a secret life. His ass was barely home because my father didn't approve of his lifestyle. He would hide the fact that he is gay. Malachi knew my dad didn't like gay people. So, he just stayed away when dad was home. My dad didn't hate him or anything. Malachi just couldn't come out the closet just yet. I loved my brother, but he needed come out in enjoy his life being gay.

"Marie, I heard you got caught with Jerome. Bitch, was the dick good?"

"Matter fact it was too damn good. I would not have gotten caught if Jerome hid in the closet. He sat his black ass on the bed. Then boom here comes granny. "

"Well, sis did you at least use a condom? I don't see no Trojan wrapper anywhere."

"I didn't use a condom. Plus, I'm ovulating today. So, in a couple of weeks, I need to take a pregnancy test. "

"Well damn, sis. I guess we both will have to miss school in go to the clinic huh."

"We don't know if I'm pregnant yet. I will have to make sure it positive first."

"Marie, bring your black ass in here right now!" my dad yelled.

I walked into the living room with Malachi behind me. I was scared shitless. I know my dad would beat my ass. Tears began to fall when I saw my dad crying. I was a daddy's girl, and it hurt knowing my father was upset with me. I had broken my dad's heart. This was a pain that I didn't want to feel at all. I hope he forgave me for what I did. I would have to gain all his trust back due to this mistake.

"Daddy, I'm sorry. Please don't hate me."

"Marie, I will never hate you. I'm not crying about you are losing your virginity. I'm crying because my little girl isn't a baby anymore. You'll be graduating soon. Well, both of my children will be. Malachi, I know you are gay. I accept you no matter what. I'm so proud of guys. "

"We love you, dad," we both said in unison.

Malachi and I ran to my dad both hugging him tight and crying. My grandmother came from her room hugging us as well. I'm so glad my family got everything together. I know we went through hard times, but the love never ended. Family always came first in my eyes. Even though my mother was no longer coming back, they were all I needed.

JEROME

*L*eaving Marie house, I was pissed. The fact we didn't use a condom pissed me off. I hope she didn't end up pregnant. I wasn't ready to be a daddy. I hope she was at least on the pill. Then her grandmother busted in on us after we finished fucking. I had to get home to rinse this sex off me. I didn't eat Marie because the bitch smelt like fish. Like her damn pH. balance was off like a muth-fucka. I thought she would at least know when she smelt bad down there. This was the worst sex experience I ever had. I should expose her fish pussy ass. I was beginning to get turned off by her ass. We had only been talking a few months though. I wanted to let her know about the issue, but that was a touchy subject to speak on. I decided to call my best friend Calvin to see what I should do.

Ring, Ring, Ring

"What's up, Rome?"

So, I just left Marie house right. We both got caught naked after we had sex. I was so embarrassed, bruh. To top that off, her pussy smelt like fish. "

"Nigga, are you serious right now? "

"Yes, nigga dead ass serious. I didn't even use a condom. So, her ass may be pregnant the way I nutted in her. I'm not ready to be a daddy, bruh."

"Well Jerome, you didn't wear a condom. What do you expect to happen if she does get pregnant? I hope you not gone tell her to abort it."

"Nigga, that's exactly what I'm going to do."

"Mane, I'll talk to you later. You are tripping, son. "

"Aight bet."

As soon as I hung the phone up, I was beyond pissed. Calvin was supposed to be on my side. How was I selfish because I didn't want to be a daddy for a child I wasn't ready for? I prayed Marie didn't end up pregnant because that would mess my life up. I wouldn't be able to attend MTSU to play basketball. I wouldn't be able to do nothing but get a damn job. I couldn't have no female mess up what I had going on. My mom would be pissed at me for getting Marie pregnant. She really didn't like her because she said that she wasn't the one for me. Her attitude was too rude and mean. I kind of agreed with my mother though. Marie had a lot of home issues she had going on.

Ding, my phone vibrated. It was Marie texting me apologizing. I just looked at and locked my phone back. This whole situation had me over the edge. I really needed to figure out what my decision was going to be with Marie. I know this would put a strain on our relationship. I couldn't handle a female with bad hygiene. It was a huge turn off for me. I always needed to hustle a lil bit of money with Braxton. Marie was not going to have this baby. I had to make sure she was pregnant first. I just had to make sure no one would find out. This was about to stress me out.

I arrived at home and noticed Braxton's car was there. He is never home this early. I wondered what the hell was going tonight. I was tired as hell, so I really didn't want to be bothered with him tonight. I walked in the house noticing Braxton weighing up some weed. I had never seen that much weed in my life. I hadn't even smoked weed before either. I wanted to ask where he got all that weed from. Why was my mother even allowing him to sell drugs in the house? I guess she didn't care because my dad was gone. My life was in shambles, and I didn't like it one bit. I walked towards my room when Braxton asked me to come here. I rolled my eyes and walked back to the living room.

"What's up, Braxton? Did you need something?"

"What's up, lil bro. I heard you got a big game on Friday. Are you ready for it?"

"Yea, I'm ready. All the scouts will be there looking me. "

"Well, I'm rooting for you. Just know if anything happens Friday, you're still great and everything happens for a reason. "

"Alright thanks, bro."

"Yea, I'm waiting on you to join the team, bro. I will have you making money. You won't even have to go to college."

"Yea, I'm good with that. I will never be another black man in the jail system."

"Aight bet."

This nigga had really lost his mind. Why would I give up college to sell some damn weed? I didn't even like the smell of weed. I wasn't going to jail for no bullshit like that. I had dreams and goals to worry about. Braxton didn't have a care for anything in the world. His biological parents were in the drug game heavy. When his dad died of drugs, he was only a few months old. Living without his father made it hard for him to adjust. I guess that's why he chose the drug game. He barely graduated high. He started selling drugs once he turned sixteen. That's all he knew was the drug game. Now that his daddy was gone, he took over what his dad left for him. I just prayed he was careful while in these streets. Lately, black men were getting killed over any and everything, but I didn't want him going out like that.

I peeked into my mom's room, and she was sleep. I'm glad she was getting her rest. Next week will be the last day she sees my dad. This divorce was taking a toll on her. After all these years, he wanted to be with a man. That just disgusted me at all cost. I was going to try in keep her level-headed while going through this. I promise when I get married I won't take my wife through this shit. Women were very precious, and they needed to be treated it like it. I know I was treating Marie wrong, but hell, I didn't want to be with her nasty ass. She needed to fix that bullshit. Just thinking about it made me gag. Maybe Friday, after this game, I would just end it with her ass, no after prom or graduation. Hell, I don't even know what I'm going to do.

I hopped in the shower to get this sex smell of me. I noticed someone else was in my bathroom. I hope damn well Braxton's baby mama Sakira wasn't here. She was eight months pregnant with his baby girl. I heard through the streets that it wasn't his child. It was his best friend Chaz's daughter. I couldn't believe it, but the truth will be out sooner than later. Shit like that doesn't keep quiet for long.

I heard her on the phone talking to someone quietly. I wonder who that person was. That bitch was sneaky as fuck, and I hated her ass. Her attitude was ghetto as fuck, and she just used Braxton for his money. I knew for a fact that she was doing something behind his back. Why hide in the bathroom to talk to someone? Females weren't shit in my eyes.

I was finally able to get in the shower when I heard the door open. I looked through the shower curtain in it was Sakira. Why the hell was she in here? I hope like hell she wasn't trying to start some shit. I wasn't up for it tonight. Her pregnant black ass needed to leave me alone. I saw her when she pulled the shower curtain back. Her eyes roamed down to my dick. I knew she wanted me to pound that pregnant pussy. I heard that shit was good anyway. This was not a good look, but hell Marie ruined it for me earlier so why not. I stepped out the shower. She removed my towel and took my dick in her mouth.

"Sakira, this ain't right girl. You're with my brother."

"Can you shut up? All I'm trying to do is give you some head. Maybe get some dick as well."

"Well, okay damn."

She began to slurp my pre-cum off my dick. She took inch by inch in her mouth. Deep throating my dick in her mouth turned me on. Sakira was a few years older than I was, but her head game was out of this world. I began to moan so loud that I couldn't contain the moans. I just hope Braxton didn't hear my young ass moaning like a bitch. If he caught me fucking his bitch, he would kill me.

"Jerome put it inside, baby love."

"I'm not about to fuck you, girl. "

"Well, let me sit on it."

She pushed me back on the toilet and sat on this long dick with no remorse. Her pussy was tight as hell. For her to be pregnant, she was fine as fuck. I shouldn't be thinking of her in that way. I was just giving her the dick in that's it. I needed to hurry up and bust this nut and go to bed. I wasn't trying to get caught in this shit.

"BOOM, BOOM, BOOM!

Braxton began to beat on the door. I was scared as hell. I didn't want him finding Sakira in here. I had to think of something quick before he walked in. I got back in the shower since the water was still running. Sakira was fixing her hair. Braxton opened the door. Whew, that was a close call. Sakira was finishing tying her hair down. Once they left out, I quickly dried off. I was never doing this shit again. My brother was a dangerous person, and I couldn't cross him like that again. Being faithful was the option for me right now.

SHAY

$\mathcal{T}$oday was the last dance show of my high school years. This moment was very bittersweet. I remembered when I first started dancing freshmen year. These years had gone too fast for me. I wasn't expecting senior year to come so quickly for me. I looked around the dance room before I went to my area to get ready. I started to tear up because this was my day to show these people that I was the one they needed. I loved dancing, and it was my life. Tonight, I would prove and take that last spot.

"Shay, it's time for us to get prepared," Alexis said.

"Alright, I'll be there in a minute."

I was headed to the dressing room when I saw Chauncey walk in with some flowers. I was literally surprised because I didn't mention anything about the dance show. He was sporting an Antioch dance shirt, black Levi's, and some Jordan Retro 11's. His hair looked freshly cut, and the cologne he had on was intoxicating. Hugging him was taking my breath away. It felt so right to be in his arms. I really was feeling Chauncey. I know we had only known each other for like three weeks, but I wanted to know about him. I know he wasn't the type that I was into, but it wouldn't hurt. I noticed he had some roses with a card as well. This was so sweet. I have never got anything special like this before. I was wondering if I even deserved this.

"Thank you for the roses. These are my favorite flowers."

"Trust, I knew that already. I noticed everything about you. I've wanted you since freshmen year, but you never gave me a chance. So, I'm trying to get a chance now before it's too late."

"What you mean before its late?"

"Well, I haven't been a great person lately, but you don't you worry about that, beautiful. You must kill this performance tonight. "

"Alright. Well, I must get dressed. I'll see you after the show."

"I hope I can take you to a nice dinner after the show. "

"Yes, you can. I'll let my granny know."

"Shay, just know you're amazing."

"Thank you. "

After he left the dance room, I quickly got dressed. My performance was third on the list. I was dancing to Beyoncé's "I Was Here" song. I loved that song. Since it would be my last night dancing, this was the best song that I could dance to. Alexis was up before me. We both had applied to the dance department at MTSU. I knew I was going to get it because I heard Alexis was late to her audition and her mouth was too smart. I watched as she danced. Alexis didn't seem like herself. She kept forgetting dance moves and just being lazy. I could tell by the judges that they weren't very impressed with her. The next thing you know she was throwing up on stage.

Was Alexis pregnant? I know her baby daddy was some drug dealer that was older than we were, but I never knew who he was. The dance instructor rushed to the dance floor to retrieve her and brought her to the dance room to lay her down. She was also foaming at the mouth. I instructed them to turn her on the side so that she wouldn't choke. I was very worried about her. I just prayed everything would be all right with her.

"Shay, it's your time to dance."

I was so excited to step on stage and do my thang. I looked through the audience in noticed my family was mid-center. I see my mother was smiling at me. I smiled and waved back. I felt the tears developing, but I began to dance to keep the tears from falling. I saw everyone smiling while cheering me on. It felt so good to hear the cheers and applauds for me after I finished. I saw Chauncey cheesing real hard when I finished my dance. I felt so accomplished afterward. I saw the people from MTSU come up to give me my award. I wanted to shout right now, but I couldn't.

"Hello Everyone Thanks for coming to the dance tonight. Before we go into intermission, I would like to present a scholarship award for dancing at MTSU. As you know, La'Shayla has been dancing since she was a freshman. She has also been co-captain of the dance team as well. I am proud to announce this $4,000 college dance scholarship to La'Shayla Nicole Barnes."

I began to cry receiving my scholarship. This was my dream since I was a younger girl. I had always dreamed of being a dancer and having my own dance studio. I saw my family come up with Chauncey following behind them. My mom kept giving me this look like she wasn't happy for me. I was trying to ignore it, but that shit was getting to me. I was trying my best to smile, but my emotions were getting the best of me. My siblings all came around to give me big hugs and tell me that I was best big sister ever. My dad and granny told me they were proud of me. Once my mama came around it was a bunch of drama.

"You didn't deserve that dance scholarship."

"Excuse me. Do you always have to start drama everywhere you go?"

"Girl, do not raise your voice at me. I hope everything goes down the drain for you. You will never be anything in life. You will be just like your no-good ass daddy of yours."

"Well, don't worry. I'll do my best to prove you wrong. Since you doubt me, that's all the motivation I need. Now if you can excuse me, I have a date to attend. "

I grabbed Chauncey's hand and walked off. I wasn't about to entertain her nonsense tonight. I was going to have a good date with my future boyfriend. My mother was very miserable with her life at this point. I will not let her determine my future. I will go to college in do everything I can do to make my family proud. I would just have to love my mother from a distance. I knew it would never be a day where our relationship would get better though. I would just have to pray for her and go about my business. There no need to keep that negativity in my life.

"Shay, are you ready beautiful?"

"Yes, I'm ready. Do you mind going to the hospital with me to check on Alexis?"

"Yea, that's cool, love. I'm pretty sure you're hungry though. I want to take you to get something to eat. "

"Alright, we can go eat first. "

Thirty minutes later, we both arrived at Wing Basket. I saw many people from school eating. I was cool with most of them but didn't really feel like talking to them. I saw a guy that looked very familiar. He was light skin with dreads hanging down his back. His lips were full and had the prettiest white teeth ever. I am staring at this man drooling from the mouth because he was fine as hell. He was just smiling while waiting for his food. My panties began to get wet just thinking about him. I was interrupted from my thoughts when they called our order number for our food. I got the food and went back to the table. Chauncey was in the restroom so waited for him to get back. I walked up to get us something to drink when the dreadlock guy came to me. I got sudden chills. He placed a small piece of paper next to me and walked off. I opened it up and read it.

Hey beautiful,

If you ever need to use this number, feel free to. Btw I'm Braxton. Jerome Brother. 615-330-2188.

I quickly place this piece of paper in my bag. I won't be using the number now but maybe for future references. Chauncey had finally made it backed to the table. He looked very worried. I wondered what was wrong with him. It looked like he had seen a ghost or something. I wondered if he knew Braxton because the way he flew to the restroom had me wondering. I could he wasn't trying to eat his food either. I had some many questions, but I really didn't want to ask him anything. I feel like it was time to end this date because he needed to clear his mind. I went and got some to go plates. I packed the food up, and we both left out.

"Are you okay, Chauncey?'

"No, that dude Braxton is after me. I stole some product from him two weeks ago."

"Chauncey, what the hell is wrong with you? You can't steal from a drug dealer. They will kill you."

"Shay, I know. That's why I must be careful. Let me get you home."

Chauncey sped to my house. I was very afraid of Chauncey going home by himself. I didn't know how Braxton was as a person. I must make sure I said a prayer for him tonight. I don't know much about drug dealers, but I know they are dangerous. I wouldn't even date one because it comes with too much stress and drama. Even though Braxton was very attractive to me, I still wouldn't date him. I just hope he didn't hurt him because I would be hurt seriously.

"Here you are, beautiful. I got you home safely."

"Thank you, love. How much do you owe Braxton?"

"Five hundred dollars."

"Wait right here. I'm about to go get the money."

"No Shay. I don't need you handling my battles."

"I'm going to be your future girlfriend, right. I got you, babe. Make sure you tell Braxton to meet you at your crib."

"Okay, babe. Thank you. Oh, and would you take the pleasure of being my girlfriend?"

"Yes, I would."

Chauncey kissed me sending chills down my spine. He gave me a feeling that I never felt before. He began to rub the inside of my thighs. I began to get hot just kissing him. My body started doing things I wasn't used to. My juice box began to get wetter than normal. He kissed my neck, which was my sensitive spot. I felt his fingers rubbing against my juice box. I didn't want to lose my virginity in this car. Just when I thought I was going to, we stopped kissing. That was an amazing kiss, but I wanted my first time to be very special. I know he felt the same way. Maybe we'd take it there the night of prom or graduation.

MARIE

a month later here I was pregnant. I was so nervous to tell my daddy and grandmother. I decided that I would wait to tell Jerome later. The only person I could tell right now is Shay. I needed to have a girl's day with her so that we can pick out prom dresses. I haven't really spoken to her since the day we got into it. I knew I was wrong because I shouldn't have blown it out of proportion. I decided I would call her in apologize to her. Regardless of how I was feeling, I needed to clear the air with my best friend. She was the person that truly knew me.

U-G-L-Y YOU AIN'T GOT NO ALIBI YOU UGLY YEA, YEA, YOU UGLY.

"Aye, shut the fuck up. Why are y'all even picking on my friend?"

"Marie, mind ya damn business. She was bothering us first."

"Chante, lie again. Every time she comes around to the park, you are pushing her out the swing or just bullying her. If I see it again, I'm beating your ass myself. Do I make myself clear?"

"Yes, it will not happen again. I'm sorry, Shay."

"It's alright."

"Thank you for taking up for me back there. I appreciate it. You are a true friend. "

"No problem. I must look out for my best friend."
"BEST FRIENDS FOREVER."

My phone started ringing taking me out of the memory from back then. Speaking of the devil, it was Shay calling me. She must've read my mind. I was smiling so hard because I missed my best friend. It had been so long since we hung out. I just hope she was available today so that we could catch up on things. I needed to talk about my situation. It was seriously stressing me the fuck out. I knew my family would be upset with me about being pregnant in high school.

"Hey Marie, what's up girl?"

"Oh, just chilling, waiting on my granny to finish cooking break-fast. What you up to, girl?"

"Girl, are you busy today? I was thinking we can go out and have some fun. I miss hanging out with you."

"No, I have nothing planned at all. You can come get me once I finish eating. "

"Okay, just text me when you ready."

"Alright, see you later."

Once I got off the phone with Shay, I got in the shower to handle my hygiene. I needed to wash my hair as well. Since it was hot outside and I wore my hair naturally, I was going to do a wash and go. Being natural was very fun because you could do different things to your hair. Thank God I was blessed with a good grade of hair. I was fully black, but people considered me a redbone. I was 5'6 and 150 pounds. I stood at 5'10 with thick thighs and a big ass. I got my hips and thighs from my mother. Now, I barely had any boobs, but since I found out I was pregnant, they were growing a bit. I felt so nauseous smelling that food in the kitchen. I wanted to throw up. I haven't even eaten anything yet. I really needed to go to the clinic today. I just didn't want anyone calling my dad to get permission. I had to figure out something because this could turn out ugly.

Walking into the kitchen, I heard my grandmother on the phone with the doctor. I saw her eyes and noticed that she was crying. I wondered what was going on because I barely saw her cry. I went to the cabinet to grab me a plate to fix my food. I tried to eavesdrop on the conversation of my granny and the doctor's office, but she went to the other room so that I couldn't hear the conversation. Since we had a house phone, I could listen to the conversation in the other room. My mouth dropped when I heard that my grandmother is suffering from breast cancer. I suddenly ran to her bedroom to confront her.

"Granny, why didn't you tell us you have breast cancer?'

"Baby girl, I'm sorry. This is very hard to deal with. I couldn't stress you guys out with my problems."

"We are family, granny. We are supposed to know everything in this house."

"Yes, we are family, but I'm not the only one that's keeping a secret either. "

I left the room after she said that. I couldn't handle the truth. I knew I would be hiding this pregnancy until I told Jerome about being pregnant. I went to the kitchen to eat the rest of my food. I was so hungry. My appetite had changed tremendously within a month. I would eat and be hungry for a good two hours after. I really wanted to have this baby, but I knew Jerome wouldn't be fond of that. With his basketball scholarship to MTSU, he would not be willing to have a child. I knew he was going to feel like I was trying to ruin his career. I couldn't go through this pregnancy by myself. I just couldn't. I didn't want to get an abortion either because I didn't believe in those.

Shay had texted me to let know she was on the way. I decided to wear some Levi jeans, a black and white Nike t-shirt, and my white Huaraches. I tried to fit in my pants, but they were a little bit too small. I guess I'll have to wear some leggings for today. I could've sworn I bought these jeans a bit bigger, but I guess not. This was very irritating because I had just purchased these jeans two weeks ago at work. Now, I wouldn't even have a chance to wear them. I was beyond annoyed. I could just take them back and buy some bigger ones.

Fifteen minutes later, Shay had arrived. I kissed my grandmother and told her I loved her. I saw Shay's car, and it was all clean and detailed. Something was different about her. She was glowing and had a lil twitch in her walk. I wonder if she and Jerome were still talking.

The only way someone would glow like that is if they were getting some good dick. I knew Shay wasn't getting any because she wasn't talking to anyone. Well, we haven't been talking lately so there was a huge possibility that she could be talking to someone.

"Hey girl, you look cute bitch!"

"Thank you, girl, you look cute yourself."

"Why are you smiling so hard? What you got going on? Who you been fucking?"

"First of all, why does everything have to be about sex with you? I'm happy that's all."

"Everything ain't about sex with me. Whose got you happy? You still talk to Jerome?"

"Marie, why the fuck would I be talking to Jerome? That's your nigga, not mine. I don't want him. I have Chauncey. Fuck Jerome. Stop being so insecure damn."

"Bitch, I thought you didn't like Chauncey and now you all up his nuts. Thank God you got someone, so you leave my nigga alone."

"Girl whatever, I'm not about to argue with about no damn nigga today. Either we're gone have a good day, or I'll leave your black mean ass here."

"I'll be nice. I got to tell you something anyway. Girl, two weeks ago me and Jerome had sex without a condom, and now I'm pregnant."

"What are going to do? No matter what we are going to the clinic right now. Marie, you need to tell Jerome."

"I will, but not right now."

We were heading to the Planned Parenthood clinic located on DB Todd Blvd. I was so nervous about this. I didn't want them to call my parents about anything. I really did need to tell Jerome about it. I just wonder if I should text or call him. Shay was on the phone with Chauncey, so I couldn't ask her right now. She was irritating me already. They both made me sick. How could they be so in love after like a month? Maybe I was hating because she finally had someone that was into her. I should be happy for her, but I wasn't. When it came to Shay, she was more attractive than me. I know she didn't have a lot of guys after her, but she still made niggas stop when she entered the room.

I didn't like the fact she and Chauncey were dating now. I had to end this shit soon. I decided to text Braxton to see if he received his money. I didn't like Chauncey because he rejected me a few months ago. Yes, I know this was petty, but hey, I had to get his ass back. I'm crazy as hell so I couldn't handle rejection at all. Now to see him with Shay just had me livid. I would be popping up to Braxton's crib a little later.

Once I got to the doctor, I stopped in my tracks because I saw Sakira and Chaz there. I'm thinking in my head why she was there with Chaz. Sakira and Braxton had been together for almost two years now. Chaz was the enemy of Braxton. That had been beefing for years now. Sakira knew that, but she was up in this clinic with Chaz. Something was telling me that baby she was carrying wasn't Braxton child. Hell, who knows because Sakira was a true hoe out here. She really wasn't the faithful type of chick. I knew she was only with Braxton for his money. The bitch didn't even work. She just waited for a nigga to give her money. I wasn't gone tell Braxton, but I was going to snap a picture for Jerome.

I had signed in and waited for someone to call me back. I saw Sakira and Chaz staring a hole through me. I knew they were both scared shitless now. I know they thought I was going to run my mouth, but I really wasn't. That wasn't my business to tell the world.

"Marie Jones?"

"Yes, I'm right here."

"Hello, I'm Nurse Cynthia, and I will be taking your vital signs today. Can I get your date of birth please?"

"My date of birth is July 10, 1992."

"Alright, are you having any pains or issues today?"

"No pains, just here to confirm my pregnancy."

"Have you already taken a pregnancy test?"

"Yes, I took one the other day. It says I was pregnant."

"Okay well take this cup in the bathroom and pee in it halfway.

There should be a place in the bathroom where you can place the cup. See you in a few minutes."

"Alright, thanks."

I headed to the bathroom to piss in this damn cup. I just hope that I wasn't that far along, or I would really be in trouble. I wasn't ready for no damn child. I would be asking the doctor about abortion options. I couldn't go through this pregnancy, I was still young, and I wanted to enjoy life. Having a baby will slow me down. I wanted to tell Jerome so bad, but I just had to do this alone. He couldn't know. I felt dumb about telling Shay, but I trusted her, so she probably wouldn't tell. She wouldn't even want me to have an abortion. This was my best option that the moment.

Knock, Knock, Knock

"Hello, I'm Dr. Phillips. I have received your pregnancy test results back. It looks like you are about twelve weeks. So, what I'll do is prescribe you some prenatal pills to your local pharmacy."

"Dr. Phillips is it possible for abortion options? I'm not ready to have this baby. "

"It is options for that sweetie. But, why would you want an abortion?

"I just don't want the baby. I'm not ready. "

"Have you talked with the child's father?"

"No, I haven't talked to him yet. I don't want him to know about this abortion."

"Well, I will be right back with the information for the abortion. "

"Thank you."

I was irritated as fuck with this doctor. She acted like she didn't understand what I was telling her. I knew that abortions could be harmful to your body, but I didn't care at this point. I just wanted my abortion. Nothing was going to stop from getting rid of this child I didn't want. I knew some people would be mad, but this was my life. I must make decisions on my own, and I was making the best decision at this moment.

"Hello Marie, I need you to sign papers regarding the procedure for this abortion. Now, are you sure this is what you want to do?"

"Bitch, yes, this is exactly what I want to do. Now give me them damn papers to sign damn."

"I'm sorry, here you go. Sign on every dotted line. Here is a gown for you to change into. The doctor and I will be back in five minutes. "

Thank God, I was able to get this procedure done today. I would finally be able to enjoy life again. I was not going to have sex for a while. I would probably get on birth control. That would be a great option for me because I didn't have this situation again. I hope this procedure went well because I was scared as hell. I heard a lot of stories about abortions and some didn't go too well. I know this prevents some of my chances of having children again but in the future, I really didn't want kids. I grabbed my phone to text Jerome.

Baby Love: Just wanted to let you know I'm pregnant.

JEROME

I was in the middle of working out when Marie texted me saying she was pregnant. I had lost my damn appetite. I couldn't even think about food. All I could think about is bringing a baby into this world. I knew having sex without a condom would lead to this. I knew I had just signed my scholarship for MTSU Blue Raiders for basketball. This would be a life-changing experience. This news was something I just couldn't believe. I was going to be a daddy. I was going to have to pick Marie up so that we could discuss this matter. I knew this wasn't her fault, but I couldn't have her raising this child by herself. I had to step up and be a man about it.

Me: Are you okay. Did you go to the doctor?

Marie: Yes, I'm here. I'll be leaving in a few. What you up to?

Me: About to leave the gym. Pull up to my house when you done. We need to have a long talk.

Marie: Okay I'll have Shay drop me off.

Me: Aight, see you then.

I was so ready to have this talk with Marie. I needed to see where her head was at with her being pregnant and all. I knew she wasn't ready for this child, but I was man enough to make it. I was going to do everything I could to make sure my child had the best

44

life. Both of my parents were there for me, so I was going to be there for my child. The only thing that was on my mind was this scholarship that I was going to have to let go. I really didn't want to, but I had a child on the way. I decided I was going to tell my mother the news later. I would have to look for a job since I wasn't going to school full time anymore. This situation really was about to have me stressed the fuck out. I needed to smoke a blunt after this news.

Me: Aye, bro. Let me get a gram of weed for $20.

Big Bro: I got you, bro. You don't ever get to pay for any weed. I'll be at the crib in a few.

Me: Aight bet.

I hopped in the shower to take care my hygiene before Marie came over. My stomach started growling. It felt like it was touching my damn back. I wanted to be high before I ate though. I guess I could take Marie to O'Charley's since it was her favorite place to go. I was excited about having this baby. It will bring so much joy in this house since my dad had left us. I just hope my mother would agree with the decision I made. She wouldn't be getting off till later this evening, so I would be able to tell her then. My mother and I could communicate with each other very well, so we wouldn't argue or anything.

Getting out the shower, I heard Braxton and Sakira come in. I needed to get in my room before Sakira started some mess again. That girl was trouble, and I needed to stay far away from her as possible. There was something off about her, but I couldn't figure it out yet. I knew Braxton's best friend Chaz and Sakira were very close lately. I didn't know what that was all about, but something fishy was going on. I didn't know if Braxton knew, but I would sure let him know what was up. I was getting dressed when Sakira bought my weed in the room. I just faced the other side of the room to avoid any contact with her ass. I really wasn't trying to have any contact with her due to what happened the last time she was here.

"Jerome, you can't speak?"

"Sakira there is nothing really we need to discuss. What happen a couple of ago should've never happened?"

"Whatever, Jerome. You liked it. You didn't even complain about it either."

"Can you please get out my room? Damn."

"Your weed is on the table."

"I know, thank you. "

Once she left the room, I rolled two blunts up. I just needed to ease my mind. I never thought I would be smoking weed again. I had to quit smoking until basketball season was over. My coach did random drug tests because if we were caught with weed in our system, then we couldn't play. I loved playing basketball, so I just didn't bother with weed anymore. I took two puffs of the weed in started feeling it. Braxton had some powerful as shit. This shit was taking all my stress away. All I needed was some bomb ass sex and head. I knew Marie wouldn't want to do anything due to her being pregnant. I guess I would hit up Alexis instead. She always would get me right when it came sex. Let me hit her up and let know I was coming through later.

Me: I'm coming through later tonight. Be ready.

Alexis: I have company. You can't come over tonight.

Me: If you are talking about Calvin, tell that nigga to the house before I get there.

Alexis: Alright, I will. We must talk anyway. I missed my period, Jerome.

Me: Well, are you sure that baby is mine? You know how you get around with different niggas.

Alexis: Fuck you, Jerome. You a real ass fuck boy. I hope you die one day.

Me: Girl shut up. See you later.

Alexis had a bad attitude, and she was spoiled. I had been fucking with her since freshmen year of high school. We had this agreement that we would be fuck buddies since she was with my best friend, Calvin. I know I was wrong for fucking his girlfriend, but hey, she said he wasn't satisfying her. She complained to me that he would cum after five minutes. I thought that shit was funny because he would always brag like he was just blowing these girls' backs out. Calvin was my boy and all, but he just couldn't a thick chick like

Alexis. Alexis was shaped like big booty Judy in that movie *ATL*. She had ass for days. She was light skin and probably about 5'8 in height. Some people would say I was breaking the guy code, but what he didn't know wouldn't hurt him. I just hope I wouldn't get caught fucking his girl. That would ruin a good ass friendship over some pussy.

I smoked the first blunt, and I heard a car pulling up to the driveway. It was Shay dropping Marie off. I must say Shay was glowing. I didn't know what happened between the last time I saw her. I wondered if she got some dick. I guess she was just happy. She looked so damn good. I just wish I had a chance with her, but that was too much to ask for. I was determined to get with her, but the only thing that was keeping me from doing that is Marie. I had to find a way to get rid of her. I couldn't do that though because she was carrying my seed. I would have to deal with her until my child turned eighteen. Just thinking about it pissed me off. I slick think she trapped a nigga. When bitches see a man with money, they wanted all parts of it. I wasn't having that shit. So, once she pops that baby out, I'm getting a DNA test. I had to make sure that baby was mine at all cost.

"Hey, baby, why you look so upset?" Marie said.

"Are you really pregnant, Marie?"

"Jerome, yes I'm really pregnant. You don't believe me?"

"Hell naw, I don't believe you. I think you trying to trap a nigga. You know I just sign to MTSU, and your ass want to be pregnant. "

"Nigga, ain't nobody tryna trap you. I don't need you to take of my child. I can do it myself nigga. Matter fact fuck you. Goodbye, Jerome."

"So now you want to leave me. It must be a lie because you are getting defensive now."

"I said, "goodbye nigga!" she yelled.

Marie and Shay had both left my crib. I knew I had upset her, but I didn't give a damn. I just didn't believe her ass. She had blown my high with that funky ass attitude of hers. I needed to do something until Alexis hit me up letting me know Calvin was gone. I guess I would take a nap until later tonight. I was very tired from that workout this morning. A nigga had been working hard lately to keep my body in shape. I had to exercise every day so that I wouldn't get lazy.

As I was walking through the house, I noticed all my tires were flat. Now, who the fuck did this shit. I knew it wasn't Marie because she had left. It had to be Alexis because she was pissed off about earlier. That bitch had some damn nerve. That's exactly why I couldn't be with her crazy ass. She always wanted to fuck up people shit. Calvin had to deal with that shit, not me.

JEROME,

YOU WOULD REGRET THE SHIT YOU SAID TO ME. I HOPE YOU GOT THE MONEY FOR THOSE SLASHED TIRES.

YOUR WORST ENEMY.

I threw that piece of paper in the trash. Fuck everybody.

SHAY

I couldn't believe how Jerome had treated Marie. That was wrong for him to do that to her. When we pulled off, she started crying hysterically. She was beyond hurt by what he said. I don't think she would trap him with a baby for his money. If he didn't want the child, he should've wrapped the shit up in the first place. I didn't want my friend going through this pregnancy alone. I would be by her side no matter what. She didn't deserve this. Niggas these days wanted the pussy but can't be a man when a girl says their pregnant. That no good bastard. I tried to comfort her, but she just wasn't letting up. I didn't know what to say, so I just headed to Cinderella's Closet to look for prom dresses. I was excited about my prom dress.

Thank God, Chauncey and I had both agreed on lavender. Lavender was my favorite color. Chauncey was going to wear a black tuxedo with a lavender vest. I decided I was going to get a simple dress. I wanted a dress with a crop top and a long skirt that flows to the ground. I was going to get me some Brazilian Body Wave hair. I wanted to style my hair half up half down. I would have this girl name Cheronda do my makeup. When I say that girl can beat a face, she could do it. My homegirl had told me about her when I took my senior pictures in the summertime. I was looking damn good in my pictures, so I knew she would have me looking like a goddess on my prom day. I was ready for this day. It was like a week away from prom. I had to make sure I had everything I needed so I wouldn't have to worry about anything on the day it is.

We had finally arrived at Cinderella's Closet, and Marie had finally cheered up a bit. I was kind of glad because I wasn't trying to be around her being sad all day. We were going to have a fun day. I missed hanging with my best friend. I know that sometimes we were busy with work and school activities, but we always needed to make time for each other. Marie usually worked on weekends and some school nights, so I wouldn't see her until she had an off day. Hopefully, this day was great without any more drama. I must've said something too quick because Alexis was walking into the store as well. I really wasn't trying to deal with her today.

"What's up, school girl? I'm glad you like taking my spot."

"I didn't take shit from you, bitch. I earned my spot on the dance team."

"Well bitch, if I weren't pregnant, that would have been my scholarship."

"Pregnant, who is the daddy?"

"You will find out sooner or later. Have a good day, girl."

"Um, whatever."

One thing I hated was a messy ass female. Alexis always wanted to stir up some shit. The main reason her ass didn't get the scholarship is because her grades and attitude. Her grades were slipping because she was too busy skipping school and class. She was thot around school. I heard so many stories regarding her that were insane. The apple didn't fall too far from the tree though because her mother was a hoe as well. Now that I think about it, I did see my dad and her mother one day. I didn't think anything of it because they worked together. I sure hope they weren't fooling around. That wouldn't be a pretty sight if it were true. I trusted my stepdad; he wouldn't do my mother that way. I know they had issues, but I pray he wasn't sleeping with Alexis' mom.

"Shay, how you like Chauncey?" Alexis asked.

"How you know about us being together?"

"Calvin told this morning. I didn't know you like niggas with horse teeth."

"Girl, get out my face with that bullshit. Why are so worried about my business. Go get you some business. I'm tired of ya ass always fucking with me. This shit will end today. Just because your ass didn't get that scholarship, you want to pick with me. If you hadn't skipped school or class, you would've had it. You're just being a hoe sleeping with other people men, and you got a man."

"Girl, you don't know anything about our relationship. All you hear is he say she say. None of that shit is true. "

"Well, if it isn't true, who is your baby daddy?"

"That's none of your business. I know who my baby father is. I don't have to explain shit to you. Let me get my dress and leave."

"Yes, go head and do that witcho scary ass. You run away from all your problems."

"Yes, whatever."

I was so glad she was gone. I saw Marie giving me an evil look, but I didn't know what that shit was about. I didn't know what she and Alexis had up their sleeve though. Marie was very quiet when she was talking to me reckless. I wondered why she didn't say anything to her. That had me wondering if something shady was going on. Usually, Marie would be trying to fight someone behind me, but today she showed me different. Her behavior towards me lately had been real funny. First, it was me going to lunch with Jerome, and then today showing me how she really felt about me. I wasn't the one to beg for friendships, but I felt like I couldn't trust her anymore. I really felt like she was doing some shady shit behind my back with Alexis. Whatever it was, I will find out eventually. I wasn't pressed about it though.

"Shay, you really didn't have to talk to her that way. What is your issue with her anyway?"

"Excuse me? You know why I don't like that girl. She hasn't liked me since I got co-captain on the dance team. Now that I earned that scholarship, she's in her feelings. I don't give a damn though. Fuck her."

"You were taking it to a whole other level. She is a cool girl. You don't even know what that girl is going through. Her mom just got fired from her job for sleeping with your dad."

"Sleeping with my dad? I don't believe that shit. Quit lying, Marie."

"Just ask you mama. She knows. I'm sorry Shay but ya daddy's a hoe. I'm leaving with Alexis. See you around. "

"See me around. What the fuck is that supposed to mean? Now you trust her friendship over mine. Fuck you, bitch. When she fucks you over, don't come back crying to me. Big ass dummy. I hate I even met ya ass. "

Marie had left out the store. I was now heated. That bitch had something coming for her ass. How could she trust that bitch as a friend? Alexis was a fraud ass bitch. I just hope she didn't get into any trouble hanging with her ass. That girl was nothing but trouble. Now I was mad at my stepdad for cheating on my mother with her mama. I was livid. I couldn't wait to confront his ass about this shit. How could my mother be so stupid? I would've put his ugly ass out my house for sleeping with people at the job. I really prayed I didn't go through anything like this. I had to get out of this store. I paid for my things and left.

Just as I was about to leave the store, I saw Chauncey rubbing Alexis' stomach. I literally stopped the car and ran towards them. I was now crying. I couldn't believe he was having a baby by her ass. This was about to be over before it even began.

"CHAUNCEY, WHAT THE FUCK IS GOING ON HERE?

"SHAY, LET ME EXPLAIN PLEASE."

"NIGGA, WHAT THE HELL DO YOU HAVE TO EXPLAIN?"

"BEFORE ME AND YOU STARTED TALKING ME AND ALEXIS WAS TOGETHER FOR LIKE SIX MONTHS. I DON'T WANT TO BE WITH HER. I JUST WANT TO BE THERE FOR MY CHILD. "

"HOW WERE Y'ALL TOGETHER WHEN SHE'S WITH CALVIN NOW. DID SHE CHEAT ON CALVIN OR SOMETHING? THIS SHIT AIN'T ADDING UP. "

"SHE CHEATED ON CALVIN. HE DOESN'T KNOW AS OF YET. "

"WELL, I'LL BE THE ONE TO TELL HIM THAT."

"WHY WOULD YOU DO THAT, SHAY? CALM DOWN PLEASE. I STILL WANT TO BE WITH YOU. "

"I DON'T WANT TO BE WITH YOU ANYMORE. FUCK YOU, CHAUNCEY!"

I began walking away with tears in my eyes. I really was feeling Chauncey, but he was about to be a father. I couldn't trust anyone at this point. Fuck everyone.

I felt him grab my arm. I wanted to resist him, but I couldn't because he kissed me. I was weak when it came to Chauncey kissing me. He walked me to the car and drove me to his place. I began to cry uncontrollably while he was driving. He stopped the car and held me tight. All this shit that was going in my life I needed a vacation. I couldn't deal with anything else because right now my life was in shambles.

ALEXIS

I know everyone is hating me right now. I really don't give a damn though. I'm Alexis Green. I'm from Atlanta, Georgia but I was raised in Nashville. I lived with my mother and my big brother Chaz. My father had died when we were very young. My mother told us he got killed during a drug deal gone bad. My dad Octavius Green was the kingpin of the city. He was from the Dominic Republic. My dad had come to the United States with his parents when he was thirteen years old. His dad, my grandfather Julio Green, was part of the mafia. Basically, they were criminals getting paid to kill the different enemies that crossed them. So, my brother Chaz and I were part of the mafia family. The only thing that was keeping us from our money is my mother, Julia Green. I couldn't stand my mother because she was very selfish.

I knew my dad had left us some money when he died, but mom spent it on herself and this new nigga she was fucking. My mom had been dating this dude she worked with for some time now. I didn't know he was at first until I caught they ass in fucking in the kitchen after school. Ever since my dad died, she was nothing but a hoe. She would have different men coming in and out the house. I lost all respect for her when she had me suck this old man dick so that she could buy this new Louis Vuitton bag. I felt so violated that I kept my door locked when I got home from school. How could you let someone offer to get head from your own daughter who was still a minor? I didn't respect her as a mother, so I called her by her first name. That bitch didn't deserve to be a mother. I hated her with everything in me.

My brother Chaz was a few years older than me. He wasn't a thug, but he was nigga in the streets. He and his best friend Braxton were into the drug game. They had been friends since we moved to Nashville. Wherever Chaz was Braxton was there. They were both two peas in a pod. The only part Braxton didn't know is that our family killed his daddy. If Braxton were to ever find that out, he would be livid. Plus, our secret relationship would also have to end. I couldn't let my family find out about me fucking the enemy. Braxton and I had been seeing each other since I was fourteen years old. He was my first for everything my first kiss, first sexual encounter, first heartbreak, and my first pregnancy. I got pregnant by him when I was fifteen years old. I didn't have the child because I didn't want my family to find out about it. If they did, I would be ship off to our country to be a damn nun. I wasn't trying to go back that there no time soon. See in our country, if you had sex before marriage, you would have to transform your whole life to be a nun. See, I loved sex too much to be a damn nun. My family was tripping for real.

"ALEXIS, COME HERE NOW!" Chaz yelled.

"First of all, why the hell you are yelling my damn name like that? I was just waking up damn."

"Girl, shut the hell up. Here is the money to get the prom stuff you need."

"Thank you, Chaz. You the best big brother anyone could ever have. "

"No problem, sis. I'm about to head out. I got some business to take care of, so please be careful. Don't be getting in any drama."

"Ain't anybody going to get in no drama? You be careful too, bro. I love you. "

"Love you too."

Once Chaz left, I texted Marie to see where she was.

Me: Hey, what you up to?

Marie: Getting ready to head to the clinic.

Me: What's wrong with you?

Marie: Girl, I may be pregnant, but I don't want this child by Jerome. He ain't shit. Ever since he signed to MTSU, he's got a big head now. Plus, I'm not ready to be a mother.

Me: I feel ya girl. I'm pregnant too. I'm ready to have this child though. I'm five months.

Marie: Well girl, what's up?

Me: I'm going to Cinderella's Closet to get my stuff.

Marie: Shay and I are going there after I leave the doctor.

Me: Well, I have a plan to piss her off. I want her to think this is Chauncey's baby. I want this bitch to suffer. I don't like her ass.

Marie: Why Alexis. That's real childish, but okay I'll play along.

Me: That a girl. You don't want people to know your secret.

Marie: Okay girl. See you later.

I'm so glad Marie agreed to play along with me so that Shay can believe my baby was for Chauncey. I really didn't know who my baby father was. I had sex with so many men that I lost count. I didn't use protection so that could be anyone's baby. The reason I wanted to blame him is because he rejected me. I wanted revenge on every nigga that did me wrong. I didn't like that bitch because even though she didn't have a boyfriend, most dudes stop what they were doing when she entered a room. She was smart and beautiful. She even was the co-captain of the dance team. I hated her because she always stole the dude I wanted and the dreams I worked hard for. It's like that bitch wouldn't even let me live. I just wanted her to move out my way.

I thought of a plan for her to lose her scholarship. I was going to put some drugs in her locker at school. That bitch didn't need that dance scholarship. I deserved it. I really didn't deserve because I skipped school three times out the week, and I also had a bad ass attitude. My attitude was due to people treating me any kind of way. I didn't like rules or being told what to do. When my dad was living, I got what I wanted. I didn't have to beg for shit. Now, I must ask my mother and brother for shit.

Lately, I had been earning extra money by being an escort— basically sleeping with men and taking their money. I had to find a way not to depend on nobody for shit. Yes, my brother gave me money, but I just put that shit in my savings account. I used the money that I got from the men I slept with and went shopping with it. I had so much shit in my room from shopping that I had to buy storage to keep most of it in. I kept the escorting thing a secret because I didn't want anyone judging me. I love sex, and I couldn't go a day without it. You could say I was a nympho. I know this wasn't a good thing, but hell, I did what I wanted. Part of it came from not having my daddy around. It hurt like hell every day to not wake up seeing my daddy in the living room smoking a cigar watching ESPN.

I was headed out the house when Jerome pulled up. That nigga always wanted to pull up without calling first. He got on my nerves with that. I wondered why that nigga was pulling up all of a sudden when I just saw his ass last night. I'm surprised he was still walking after I sucked the soul out of him. That nigga knew he loved some head from me. Thankfully, my older men I fucked with taught me how to suck a mean dick. Giving head was one of my favorite things to do. I'll have a nigga weak as hell after I was done. Every nigga wished I were their wife, girlfriend, side bitch, sister, mother, grandmother, and baby mama. I had the best head around.

"Alexis, where are you about to go?"

"I'm going to Cinderella's Closet."

"So is this child really mine. I know ya ass is a lil escort in shit. So, any nigga you fucked could be the daddy. So, when you have this bastard baby, I need a DNA test."

"You weren't saying that shit last night. Now you want to come to my crib talking reckless. Nigga, get the fuck off my porch. "

"Bitch, you still a hoe. Calvin got him a hoe ass girlfriend. I bet he doesn't know my dick been down your throat, does he? See you around Alexis."

"Fuck you, bitch."

57

When Jerome pulled off, I was hurt by what he said. It was true I was a hoe. I couldn't just be with one nigga. I couldn't commit to any nigga. Niggas weren't shit. The reason for this is because Braxton cheated on me and left me for this bitch name Sakira. That bitch stole my man from me. Sakira was supposed to be my best Friend, but she was fucking my man behind my back. See, Sakira was in a bad environment at home, so I let her stay with us until she got on her feet. I trusted her to be around Braxton, but then she began to catch feelings for him when I wasn't around.

I didn't know until he broke up with me during a text message after I got off work. We had been texting all day like we normally do, but he hit the bomb on me. I was devastated and so hurt. I had done everything for that man. I bought him everything he wanted from shoes, game systems, going on trips, and just making sure he stayed happy. I thought I everything he wanted, but that was untrue. I was wondered what he saw in her, and what he didn't see in me. Ever since we broke up, my heart hasn't healed. I get with different men to ease the pain. I feel like when I shop it makes me forget about everything going on in my life.

I was on the way to Cinderella's Closet when my irking ass boyfriend called me. Calvin was a good dude, but he wasn't good for me. He spoiled me with everything that I wanted, but his dick just wasn't pleasing to me. He reminded me of Chicago in *Poetic Justice*. He had that same old tired ass haircut like him to. That shit got on my nerves. I told him several times to cut that bullshit off, but he never did. Calvin was just a nigga to be around when I wasn't getting love from anyone else. I was just using him to get what I wanted, and then I'll be dumping his ass.

I finally pulled up to Cinderella's Closet when I see Marie and Shay walking towards the store. I couldn't wait to get under this bitch skin. She always wanted to take everything that was mine. I wanted to ruin this bitch life every chance I got. I got out the car so that I could mess with her. This was going to be funny to me.

"What's up, school girl? I'm glad you like taking my spot. "

"I didn't take shit from you, bitch. I earned my spot on the dance team."

"Well bitch, if I weren't pregnant, that would have been my scholarship."

"Pregnant, who is the daddy?"

"You will find out sooner or later. Have a good day, girl."

"Um, whatever."

Shay was right I didn't know my baby father was. I was still trying to figure that out. Jerome didn't believe my ass at all. He knew I was lying about this baby being his. When we had sex, he had wrapped it up. I just cut a hole in the condom before I slipped it on. I wanted to trap him because he had just signed to MTSU. I thought that would be a great idea because he would be earning lots of money in the future. I just saw him as a person to raise my child, which means that would have everything they needed.

Bringing me out of crazy thoughts, I overheard Shay and Marie talking about some guy she was dating. Calvin had already told me that she was dating Chauncey anyway. I just always wondered what he saw in her that he didn't see in me. I was jealous of her, but it wasn't a reason to be. I just didn't like her because she was better than me. No way saw any wrong in her. That's exactly why I was going to get Marie to help me with this plan when we get back to school. I was going to ask Chaz for the drugs so that I can place them in her locker and get that scholarship I want. I hope this plan works because I need to show my family I can get into college and succeed. I walk towards them so that I can get Marie to leave with me to talk about this plan I had.

"Shay, how you like Chauncey?" I asked.

"How you know about us being together?"

"Calvin told this morning. I didn't know you like niggas with horse teeth. "

"Girl, get out my face with that bullshit. Why are so worried about my business. Go get you some business. I'm tired of ya ass always fucking with me. This shit will end today. Just because your ass didn't get that scholarship, you want to pick with me. If hadn't skipped school or class, you would've had it. You just being a hoe sleeping with other people men and you got a man."

"Girl, you don't know anything about our relationship. All you hear is he says/she says. None of that shit is true. "

"Well, if it isn't true who is your baby daddy?"

"That's none of your business. I know who my baby father is. I don't have to explain shit to you. Let me get my dress and leave."

"Yes, go head and do that witcho scary ass. You run away from all your problems."

"Yes, whatever."

I walked out of that store feeling good. Marie and Shay were going at it. I knew felt a little bit of betrayal, but I didn't give a damn. I saw Chauncey pulling up when I was walking out. This would be a great time to frame him for my pregnancy so that she could get mad and run off. This shit was going to be hilarious. I walked towards him and grabbed his dick. He was so damn fine. I was getting aggravated that he kept pushing my hand away. I just wanted his ass to want me like I wanted him. It was just too hard for me to get him at his weakest point. I had to think of a plan for his ass too. I wanted everyone to go down.

Suddenly I saw Shay running outside the store mad and crying. I looked at Marie who was kind of sad. That bitch had better not back out of this shit now if she wants that money. I had promised her five stacks if she helped me with my plan. She had another thing coming if she thought I was doing this alone. Shay finally made it towards Chauncey and me. I was standing there with my resting bitch face. I didn't have a care in the world.

"CHAUNCEY, WHAT THE FUCK IS GOING ON HERE?"

"SHAY, LET ME EXPLAIN, PLEASE."

"NIGGA, WHAT THE HELL DO YOU HAVE TO EXPLAIN?"

"BEFORE YOU AND I STARTED TALKING, ALEXIS AND ME WERE TOGETHER FOR LIKE SIX MONTHS. I DON'T WANT TO BE WITH HER. I JUST WANT TO BE THERE FOR MY CHILD. "

"HOW WERE Y'ALL TOGETHER WHEN SHE WITH CALVIN

NOW. DID SHE CHEAT ON CALVIN OR SOMETHING? THIS SHIT AIN'T ADDING UP. "

"SHE CHEATED ON CALVIN. HE DOESN'T KNOW AS OF YET. "

"WELL, I'LL BE THE ONE TO TELL HIM THAT."

"WHY WOULD YOU DO THAT, SHAY? CALM DOWN PLEASE. I STILL WANT TO BE WITH YOU. "

"I DON'T WANT TO BE WITH YOU ANYMORE. FUCK YOU, CHAUNCEY!"

I wanted to laugh at this bitch so bad. She needed an Oscar the way she was acting. I saw Marie laughing at her ass. I wanted to laugh, but I had to keep a straight face. I wanted her to see that I didn't care how she felt. I wanted her to feel the pain that I was feeling. I wanted that bitch to suffer just like me. I bet she wouldn't want him after this stunt. She ran off crying just like a little ass girl would to her mama when she fell off a bike. I got mad when I saw Chauncey ran after her. He was supposed to be there to comfort me, not that bitch. I saw he had kissed her and almost gagged because he was being weak for her. That's probably why I couldn't be with him.

"Marie, bitch, come on we got shit to do."

"Alright, are you sure about this?"

"Hell yea, I'm sure. You should be as well. I'm the one giving you the five stacks, bitch."

"Okay, let's get this done."

"That's what I'm talking about."

MARIE

I was so glad that we were leaving Cinderella's Closet. I felt so bad about treating Shay that way. We had been friends for so long. I knew it would be a bad idea for me to this plan with Alexis, but I needed this money. I liked hanging with her and being around her. I knew I shouldn't be trusting her over my best friend, but I had to do this for me. I needed this money to pay for school and any other things I needed for school. I knew I was putting my life in danger messing with this knowing her family was part of a mafia family. I just prayed that I didn't get myself in any deep trouble fooling with her. I was ready to get this shit over with. I was stressing over this shit. I had other things to be worried about.

"Marie, where do you want to eat?"

"I'm not really hungry."

"Bitch, shut up, you haven't eaten since this morning. We are going to Five Guys. I'm craving a burger. "

"Alright, that's fine with me."

"Why are you acting so nervous? You will be alright. We are not going to get caught, girl. I got this I promise."

"I sure do hope so. I have been stressed since we talked about the shit."

"Girl quit worry and trust me. "

Fifteen minutes later, we had arrived at Five Guys in Smyrna. I hadn't had this in so long. I barely even came here due to the prices being so damn high. I was always eating off the kid's menu.

I must've been hungry because my stomach started growling. I was very hungry after that procedure I had done. I was kind of was feeling guilty about what I did. I really didn't care though. For Jerome to stay with me, I was going to fake this pregnancy good. I didn't know why I wanted to lie about this pregnancy, but I was forced to do it. Alexis wanted me to get pregnant with her. The night Jerome and I had sex couple of months ago I poked a hole in his condom. She didn't want to be pregnant by herself, so she paid me to become pregnant. Little did she know, I had already got an abortion. I didn't want to be a mother. I wanted to go to college and live my life. I will have to create a big ole ball to make it look like I'm pregnant. All I needed was the money. I think I would have to fake a miscarriage so that she could believe I lost the baby. I couldn't let her find out about this abortion because she would probably kill me.

When we walked in Five Guys, we had spotted Calvin and Jerome together. They both looked at us with mugs on their faces. It wasn't a good look at all. Alexis looked at me with tears in her eyes. She knew what this was all about. I got pissed because I was mixed up with this shit. I knew she had lied to the both about being the daddy to her unborn child. Calvin was so upset at her. I really didn't want to be here if something popped off. I said a little prayer that everything would be alright. I glanced at Alexis who looked scared like a child without their mother, so I went over to the table to comfort her.

"Alexis, so is this Jerome's baby?" Calvin asked.

"No, it's not his baby or your baby. I don't know whose baby it is."

"Damn, I was being loyal to ya hoe ass. I had millions of chicks after me, but I was being loyal to you. This shit hurts so much. I thought you were going to be one I married. I can't do this shit no more. It's crazy because I had a feeling you were out doing something. I would call you at night, but you would never answer. I used to find your location, and you were always at a hotel. "

"Man, stop lying. Who you been talking to?"

"Alexis, I haven't been talking to no one. I did this investigation myself. I used to follow you some nights when you wouldn't answer me. You would always blow me over. I'm tired of this. To know that the baby isn't mine is very heartbreaking as well."

"So, what now you want to break up with me. You have been listening to all these niggas. You haven't even tried sitting down to talk to me, Calvin."

"I don't want to talk about anything with your ass. We are DONE!"

"No, Calvin please don't leave me. I need you, Calvin, please. Just give me another chance."

"There aren't any more chances. I'm going to the Navy after graduation. Goodbye, Alexis."

"This isn't fair. I love you, Calvin. Please don't leave me."

Calvin left Five Guys like a mad raging bull. He was so pissed off. I had never seen him this mad before. Alexis knew she was wrong for doing him that way. I understand some folks may get unhappy, but why do folks cheat? It just reminded that she was going to frame Jerome for the baby. I wondered what all that was about. I needed to get down to the bottom of this. Why was she trying to frame Jerome? I wasn't going to ask them now, but eventually, I would. I had to stick with the plan. I couldn't blow because I know her ass wouldn't give me my money. I grabbed her off the floor and took her to the restroom. She was starting to stink with that throw up on her. I hated the smell of throw up.

"Alexis, come on so that you can get cleaned up."

"Marie, just let me sit here. You can leave. "

"Girl, I'm not about to leave you here by yourself. Look, I will take you home if you want me to."

"Alright, just take me home. I need to get some rest."

"Are you okay? I'm sorry about you and Calvin."

"Why the fuck are you sorry? You didn't do anything. I did this to myself. Now, I'm out a prom date. "

"So, is it true that you and Jerome had sex?"

"Bitch, no we didn't have sex. Don't believe everything you hear."

"Well, I was just checking girl. Don't get all feisty with me."

"Yea whatever, you can leave now."

I didn't like how that bitch was coming at me. I was going to watch her very closely. She could be very sneaky at times. I kept my composure because I would've snatched that bitch up quick. I don't tolerate disrespect well. I got and left. I saw Jerome standing outside smoking some weed. I wondered when he started smoking. I looked at him his vibe was very off. I wanted to bring the situation up with Alexis, but I declined. I didn't want to start any drama with him. Looking at him smoke that blunt made my pussy wet. I haven't had no dick since I found out I was pregnant. I walked towards him and put my tongue down his throat. We kissed passionately in the parking lot. Then he stopped quickly. I looked kind of confused because he was acting differently. I didn't know what his issue was, but I was ready to go home.

"Can you take me home, please?"

"Yea, I got ya."

"Why are you acting so nonchalant, Jerome? Is something bothering you?"

"I need some space to think. It's nothing against you, babe."

"Alright, if you need anything I'm here."

"Thank you."

JEROME

When I left Five Guys, I was pissed off. I couldn't believe Alexis was trying to frame me for that pregnancy. That bitch was out of her mind. I knew she was a hoe from when I met her. I just wanted the pussy. I felt bad for my homie Calvin though. He was out here being faithful to a hoe. It seems that the niggas that treated females' right, they get treated wrong. I was different from most niggas though. I couldn't just commit to one female. I had to keep at least three or four females by my side. My motto was if one acts up, I can go chill with the next one. I know that sounds fucked up, but hey, I couldn't stand these females with attitude and always wanted to nag about something. I hated that shit.

Marie tried to get me to open up to her, but I couldn't do that shit. I knew she was having my seed, but that bitch was getting on my nerves. When I saw her hanging with Alexis, I knew something was up. I wanted to ask her why she was hanging with her anyway. I knew she had paid Marie to do something crazy with her. For Marie to be hanging with Alexis, she had to be getting some type of money out of it. I was going to find out about it eventually. I wanted to spoil her to at least get some answers out of her. I needed to know if that bitch was having my baby. If I found out that she wasn't having my child, it would be hell to pay.

"Marie, when did you start hanging with Alexis? I heard about what happened at Cinderella's Closet today."

"I mean damn is it a crime to hang with her. What has she done to you?"

"Man quit with the attitude, bruh. I was just asking a damn question. That's exactly what I am talking about. You have a nasty attitude, bruh. I try to do something nice for ya funky ass, but you always ruin the shit. "

"My attitude is because I'm hungry. I haven't eaten all day. Are you gone feed me or what?"

"I'm going to take you somewhere to eat. But first, you got to tell me something. Are you really pregnant with my child, Marie?"

"Yes, I'm pregnant with your baby. You think I would lie about having a child. That's real bogus of you, Jerome."

"Look, man. I have a scholarship to play ball. I ain't tryna be nobody daddy right now. Ya ass should've taken them birth control pills. I slick think you tryna trap a nigga."

"Nigga, trap you? Why the hell would I trap you? We both laid down in made this baby. I didn't make this baby by myself, nigga."

"Girl, I'm taking your ass home. I can't even have a decent conversation with you because of your fucked-up attitude. "

"Fuck you. I'll be glad to go home and call my other nigga," she said while laughing.

I pulled the car over as soon as her funky pussy said that. I was mad as hell. Why would she bring up another nigga? I suffered from a mild case of being bipolar. I didn't like shit like this. I was a jealous nigga as well. I didn't like another nigga around my bitches I fuck with. I sat there a minute to calm down, but I couldn't. I looked over at her with that big smirk on her face. That bitch just didn't know I was about to beat her ass some serious. I didn't tolerate disrespect. Marie knew damn well I didn't want her around any other niggas but me. That probably wasn't even mine since she mentioned it.

"Jerome, Cheer the fuck up. I was just playing take a damn joke, geesh."

The next thing I knew I was holding to her neck so tight. I wanted to kill that bitch off. I could see her face turning red. She was very light skin, so I knew these grips from my hands would be on her neck. I could tell she was trying to say something, but I continued to choke her. Catching me off guard her phone started ringing. I saw this nigga name Quinn pop up. I bet this was the nigga she was talking about. I wanted to be home so that I could talk to this nigga. I quickly drove home. I lived right around the corner from Five Guys anyway. I jumped out the car and ran into my house. Her ass was still in the car crying. I didn't give a fuck because she brought this on herself.

I called this nigga Quinn back. He didn't answer when I called the first time. I went to my room to grab my blunt. Walking out of my room, that nigga Quinn was calling her phone back. I answered on the first ring.

"What up, lil nigga. Why are you calling my girlfriend? She belongs to me. She is not allowed to have any male friends. I'm her only friend."

"Listen here, nigga. I'm the wrong nigga to be getting loud with. Marie and I have been best friends for over five years now. You can't break with this bond we have. "

"Nigga I can break whatever bond y'all think you will continue. I don't play about my women."

"Your women? See you a dog ass nigga. Why you got to have other bitches when you got her?"

"Don't worry about all that. Just don't ever call this number again."

"Aight bet."

Once I got off the phone with that nigga, I went back outside. I unlocked the car door. I grabbed her arm and dragged her out the car into the house. She was doing all that whining and crying asking me to stop. At this point, I was hurt and mad. I couldn't believe her. I looked at her she was still beautiful while crying. I didn't want to hit her, but the way my anger was setup I wanted to show her who's boss.

"Who is that nigga Quinn to you, Marie?"

"He is my best friend, Jerome. I told you about him when we first got together."

"I don't recall you ever telling me about no nigga Quinn. You probably were lying because I don't believe you."

"Well, you don't have to believe me. Why are you so damn insecure? For someone to be a future pro basketball player, you have a lot of insecurities and anger issues."

"WHAT THE FUCK DID YOU JUST SAY, BITCH?"

"NIGGA, YOU GOT ONE MORE TIME TO CALL ME A BITCH. I DON'T KNOW WHAT HAS GOTTEN INTO YOU, BUT I'M NOT THE ONE."

SLAP!

"JEROME, WHAT THE FUCK IS WRONG WITH YOU?" YOU BITCH ASS NIGGA. NO REAL NIGGA PUT HIS HANDS ON A FEMALE. "

I pushed her against the wall and started punching her ass in the face. I could feel the blood running down my hands. I took her to the bathroom to show her what I was about to do with her phone. I was going to flush that bitch in the toilet, so she wouldn't be able to talk to no one. I looked at her with all that blood on her face. I didn't understand why she wanted to see this side of me. I hated bringing this side out at times. I heard someone opening the front door. I pushed her inside my room in locked the door. I rinsed my hands off to avoid showing evidence of what happened.

I walked into the living room, and it was Braxton coming home. I was scared as hell because I didn't want him seeing Marie beat up. Next thing I know Marie started yelling help crying in shit. Braxton looked at me confused.

"Bro, who the fuck is that yelling? What did you do? Why is blood on your shirt?"

"Um, that's Marie yelling. We kind of got into an argument."

"Did you hit her, bro?"

"Yea, I did. I flushed her phone down the toilet. "

"Why the hell would you do that? Your ass is going to jail."

"Naw bro, I can't go to jail. I have a career. I can't fuck this chance up."

"Nigga, go get that girl out that room. Let her get cleaned up so that I can take her home."

"Alright, bro."

I went to my room to get Marie so that she could go home. I knew I had fucked up for putting my hands. I hope she didn't get the police involved in this situation. I know domestic violence charges weren't anything to play with. I walked into the room she was sound asleep. I didn't want to touch and make her think that I was going to hit her again. I walked over to her in tapped her to see if she would wake up. She instantly woke up, and her face was fucked up. It was black and purple all over. Blood was smeared across her nose. Her neck looked horrible I could see my fingerprints all over it. I felt so bad. I had let my anger get the best of me. The girl I was supposed to have loved for was bruised up because of me.

"Marie, my brother volunteered to take you home."

"Can I use the phone, please? I need to call someone."

"Yea, the phone is in the kitchen. "

"Alright."

While Marie was using the phone, I fired up a blunt. I was stressed as hell. I can't believe my anger got the best of me. I shouldn't have put my hands on her. No matter how mad I got, I should've kept my composure. My mother always told me never to put my hands on a woman. If she found out about this, she would be very upset. See my mother had a high standard for me. She always bragged about me to her friends. I prayed to God Marie didn't call the police. I didn't want to be involved with no police. Police were snakes these days. They would lie about anything just to look good. I didn't want to be a young man in the category like the rest of them.

I walked into the living room noticing the police were already outside my house. I couldn't believe this shit was happening. I didn't want to go to jail for my actions. This was some bullshit. I looked at the time in my mother would be home any minute. I just hope she didn't arrive when the police were here. I would be in some deep shit.

My mother didn't like the police at her house simply because the attention they brought in the neighborhood.

Knock, Knock, Knock!

"Hello Officer, how can I help you, sir?

"Well, it seems that you got some charges against you. We got a call stating that you beat Ms. Marie until she was black and blue."

"We got into a heavy argument, and I let my anger get the best of me."

"Well, you know putting your hands on a woman is not the solution when you get angry. She stated will wants to file a restraining order against you. That means she doesn't want you near her."

"She is my girlfriend though. How will I able to be away from her?"

"Like I said, stay away from her. Have a good day, sir."

Once the police left, all I could do is smoke. I couldn't think straight. I needed to release some stress. I decided to hit up Felicia. She was a girl I would hit up when I needed some pussy. Felicia and I had been messing around since like the eighth grade. I could always count on her when I needed her.

"What's up, Jerome?"

"I need to release. I'll be there in a few."

"Alright, I'll be here."

SHAY

*W*e had arrived at Chauncey house. I was so hurt. Alexis really had me thinking that was his child. I should've known she was lying. That girl was a true hoe. She was an escort. She would fuck any man with a dick. I stand her ass. I was mad at Marie. I couldn't understand how she could be on Alexis' side instead of mine. I had a feeling she was forced to do something crazy for Alexis to be cool with her. See, she would manipulate people to get what she wants. If she didn't get what she wants, then she would threaten to kill you. I decided to hit Marie up to see what she was up to. I needed to find out what was up with her.

Me: What's up girl? Is there a way we can talk?

Best friend: Hey, Jerome and I just got into an argument. He put his hands on me. I have blood all over my face. I'm all black and blue. Braxton is taking me to the urgent care clinic now. I put a restraining order out on him.

Me: OMG are you serious? Which urgent care are you going to? Chauncey and I can meet you there if you want us to.

Best friend: Yes, I would love for you to come with me. I gotta tell you everything that happened anyway.

Me: Text the details of the place.

Best friend: Thank you; see you when you get here.

I was damn near in tears when Marie told me Jerome put his hands on her. I wondered how that felt to not have someone there to protect you from someone like that. I never thought he would ever do that to her. You never know what someone may do until you with them. That's why I was guarding my heart when it came to Chauncey. I was feeling him and all, but I had to watch his actions. Actions speak louder than words to me. I'm glad he was very patient with me though. He wanted to get to know me for me. He didn't even pressure me into anything I didn't want to do. I was very grateful and appreciative of that as well.

"Chauncey!" I yelled.

"Babe, why are you yelling at me?"

"We have to leave. Marie is on the way to the urgent care. "

"Why, what's wrong with her?"

"Apparently Jerome decided to be a boxer by punching her all over her face."

"Are you serious?"

"Yes, so hurry up and get dressed."

"Aight, I'll be ready in five minutes."

Five minutes later, Chauncey had come back in the living room looking fine as hell. For someone who was just putting on some clothes, he made it look real sexy. I glanced at him in my pussy started getting moist. I started twitching from left to right to ease my vagina's heartbeat from throbbing. I wanted him inside me so bad. Now, I wasn't a virgin, but the first time it was horrible. I began to think naughty.

I knew it was too early to having sex with Chauncey, but I was feenin'. I needed to feel something hard against my soft, gentle fold. I guess he was feeling the same way because he came over to me kissing me passionately. I felt his dick press against my ass. He placed his fingers inside my panties while rubbing my clit at the same time. Good thing I had on a dress because it was easy for him to reach my hole. He places two fingers inside of me. He pumped both fingers in and out, and that shit was feeling amazing. He pulled me closer to him kissing my lips. Moving down to my neck, he began to bite my neck, which turned me on. I let out a soft moan letting him know it felt great. We kissed again like first time lovers on their first date.

Chauncey began to admire me from afar while he took his clothes off. I began to get nervous with the way he was staring me. No one had ever looked at me the way he did. I removed my blue bodycon dress. He licked his lips as he admired my body with just my bra and boy shorts on. He came closer to me kissing me again so passionately. I began to get moist feeling his hardness press against my inner thigh. I pushed him against the couch so that I could straddle him. Chauncey slid himself inside of my wetness. I took deep breaths as he slid each inch in little by little. I began to move my body slowly as I got used to the size. For him to be slim and tall, he was working with a monster. I grabbed the couch as I rode him slowly, up and down, round and round as his thickness began to fill my wetness. As I continued to ride him, I heard someone coming inside the house. We didn't bother to see who came inside. I was just enjoying the moment. I heard someone getting closer to the living room. I began to slow the pace down. His moans began to grow louder as I clenched my walls even tighter.

"Shay, damn baby you can't be clenching your walls like that. You gone make me bust too quick."

"Nigga, just fuck me damn. I'm trying to get my nut too, damn."

"Oooh you feisty, I love that shit, girl."

"Well, daddy, give me my dick."

Chauncey thrusts began to get faster as I rode him faster. I began to feel myself trying to release, but I didn't want to release yet. I turned around so that he could give it to me doggy style. That was my favorite position. I felt like I had all type of control throwing it back against him. Just letting him know that I had control gave me life. I went to work as soon as he slid that dick in. I began to bounce my ass harder against his dick. I felt his dick growing even more as I kept bouncing on his pole. As he pushed me back down so that I can arch my back, He went deeper and deeper as he felt his about to release.

"Oooh baby, I'm about to cummmm!"

"I'm about to cummmm too, baby!"

Chauncey released inside of me since he knew I was on birth control. We both took deep breaths as we lay down beside each other. It felt so good as we pulled each other closer together. I began to play in his hair while he kissed me softly on my lips.

"Shay," Chauncey said while getting a towel to clean us up."

"Yes," I replied while looking at my phone.

"Aren't we late meeting Marie at the clinic? I hope she doesn't get mad at us. "

"Boy, she will be alright. It has been plenty of times where she had me waiting on her."

Chauncey came over to me with the hot towel to clean my insides. "Shay I promise I will never do anything to hurt you. I will always keep this pretty smile on her face. "

"I promise I will do the same for you, baby. I'm your ride or die. I'm your Bonnie, and you're my Clyde. I leaned against his chest while giving him more tongue. I didn't want to start another round, so I quickly got dressed.

* * *

CHAUNCEY and I walked into the clinic located on Murfreesboro Road called United Health Works. It was a walk-in clinic that treated for mostly everything. It was a little different from most clinics, but it will do for now. I glanced around to see if Marie was sitting in the lobby. I saw her sleeping near the window. I saw my best friend, and I couldn't believe what I saw. Her face didn't even look the same. I felt bad because I wasn't there for her when she needed me. Chauncey had finally come back from using the restroom when he saw me crying. He wrapped his arms around me. He was just the person I needed to comfort me.

Marie's face looked very bruised up. Her face was red and purple, and her nose was all busted up and bruised. Everything on her face was beaten up. She looked like a totally different person. This wasn't the person I knew. She was the person that would always take up for me. Now it was me that had to protect her from someone. I just wondered how long Jerome had been putting his hands on my friend. These were the things that I needed to know. I just knew she might not want to tell me her business, but for her to get the help she needed to tell me everything. I just prayed that she would get through this situation. I couldn't imagine losing her due to domestic violence. From this day forward, I was going to protect her.

I walked over to where she was sitting. I tapped her tad to see if she would wake up. She appeared a bit a frightened when I touched her. She began to look around to see if Jerome was around. I began to worry because I didn't want her living out of fear. I really hope she put that restraining order out on him because she was going to need it. I examined her from head to toe, and she was really damaged because of this. I never understood why men put their hands-on women. I guess they lacked in other places so putting their hands-on women made them have a lot of control.

"Marie, are you alright?"

"Does it look like I'm alright?"

"No, I'm sorry for asking that dumb ass question. I'm sorry this happened to you, girl."

"No need to be sorry. I got myself into this situation. He beat my ass because of my best friend called me."

"So, he must've got jealous?"

"Yes, he did. He flushed my damn phone down the toilet, so I have no phone to contact anyone."

"Well, I have my old iPhone 6 Plus you have since I purchased my iPhone 7 Plus last week. "

"Matter fact once we leave we can go get it. Marie, I want you staying with me until everything clears over."

"Alright, I can do that."

* * *

THIRTY MINUTES LATER, we were leaving the clinic. Marie had a fractured jaw and some broken bones in her arm. I felt so sorry for her.

The only thing she needed from me is support and comfort. I had already let my parents know that she would be staying with us for a while. Her dad and grandmother had called to make sure she was in good hands. I let them she just needed some space and time. I told them to not worry about anything. I had Chauncey to pick up some food and movies. We were going to chill tonight. It wasn't anything going on tonight anyway. I could tell Marie was good and comfortable because she was smiling while giving us some conversation. I couldn't believe in a few weeks we were going to be graduating. This would be a bittersweet moment.

MARIE

Three Weeks Later

I heard my ringtone going off for the third time. It was my ex-boyfriend Jerome calling me apologizing again. I didn't want to hear anything he had to say. As you may know three weeks ago, we got into an altercation. Jerome basically got jealous because my best friend Quinn called me. Quinn and I didn't have anything going on, but I did have some feelings for him. I didn't want Jerome to know that because he would go after him. I had known Quinn from growing up in church. He was the grandson of my granny's best friend. We had always been close since preschool. I never did take it that route with him because I didn't want to ruin the friendship. If I ever needed him, he was always there.

My phone rang again. I contemplated on answering it. I had filed a restraining order on him so that I couldn't have any contact with him at all. I was still staying at Shay's house, so I didn't need no extra attention on me.

Jerome: Hey Marie. I'm so sorry. I didn't mean to put my hands on you, babe.

Me: Jerome look, I don't have anything to say to you. My jaw was fractured, and I had a few fractured bones in my ribs. I'm just now fully healed from all that shit. I'm still damaged from what you did. Just leave me alone, please. I trusted you with my heart, and you stepped on it.

Jerome: Well, can I see you? These three weeks have been sickening not being able to talk to you.

Marie: When are you trying to see me, Jerome? I'm not trying to be seen with you or around you. I'm kind of staying with Shay now.

Jerome: Just meet me at the corner by my house. Please come by yourself.

Marie: See you in fifteen minutes.

I felt kind of stupid for answering his texts. I had to figure out a way for me to get away from Shay for like an hour. I knew she would have many questions to ask before I left. I would just lie and say I needed to get some air and come back. I hated lying to my friend, but hell, what can I say I missed him as well. I knew he bout damn killed me, but I still loved him. Here I was trying to make excuses for him, but I needed to feel his touch. Not being able to see him for these three weeks was pure hell. Shay was always checking my phone to make sure I wasn't giving into his lies. She never found anything because I deleted everything before she could even find something. I knew the truth would eventually come out, but I didn't care.

Twenty minutes later, I had arrived in front of Jerome's house. I was so glad Shay believed my lie. I had told her I was going to the store to get a few things. I hope she just didn't follow me behind. I was so worried about meeting up with him though. My hands were sweaty, and I felt hot suddenly. I was so worried about getting caught that I didn't see Jerome standing there. I contemplated on opening the door. I took three deep breaths in finally opened the door up. He grabbed my hand to help me out the door. I glared at him up and down, which he looked a bit different from three weeks ago. Jerome looked thin, and his hair was all over his head. I kind of felt bad for putting him through this though. I should've just kept my mouth closed. I guess I was in love because I keep forgetting he did put his hands on me. It wasn't a good sign by him putting his hands on me. I just needed to leave him alone altogether. I don't know what it was, but I just couldn't leave him alone.

"Jerome, why do you look like you lost your first puppy?"

"I have lost someone very special to me because of my dumb mistake."

"Why did you have to put your hands on me?"

"I lost control of my anger babe. I promise you it will never happen again, Marie. Can you please give another chance to prove myself?"

"You will have to show me. Actions speak louder than words."

"Well babe, can I at least show you I've changed please?"

"Yea, I guess so."

We both walked into his house to chill. He had turned on Netflix to find a movie. It was some movie called *Mississippi Damned*. The movie was about a Mississippi family tragic cycle of abuse, addiction, and violence leaves three poor black siblings from rural Mississippi with a choice between confronting the curse that's plagued their family for generations and succumbing to the grim fate that threatens to seal their legacy. The movie had me all in my feelings. I began to cry uncontrollably when I saw the man slap his pregnant wife. I knew then it was time for me to leave. I couldn't sit there and watch that when I just when through the same situation three weeks ago. No matter how I felt about Jerome, he was wrong for putting hands on me. I must accept the fact that he was wrong, and it wasn't my fault. I kept blaming myself for this matter. It hurt, but I needed to stay away from him before I ended up hurt.

Buzz, Buzz, Buzz!

I glanced at my phone noticing Shay had messaged me.

Shay: *Making sure you're okay. Chauncey and I are picking up some Wing basket. Want something?*

Me: *Just get me a seven-piece original hot combo please with extra fries and a Dr. Pepper. Thank you.*

Shay: *No problem.*

Jerome was staring a hole through me while texting Shay. I knew he was irritated. I decided that it was time for me to leave before something occurred again. I got up from the couch while gathering my things to leave. I avoided letting him know that was I was heading back to Shay house. Not even halfway through the door, I felt his hands around my neck. I said a silent prayer that I got out here safely.

Dear God,

I know I haven't talked to you in a while, but can you please get me out here safely.

"Marie, so you just gone leave me without giving me a reason? I'm supposed to always know where you are."

"Jerome, I don't have to be around you all the time for you to know about your unborn child. Right now, it's not safe for me to be around you. I should've just stayed where I was."

"Alright well, I let you have your space then. My number is always available if you need me. "

"Jerome please get it together. Don't be blaming everyone for your mistakes."

"Alright, see you around."

ALEXIS

That day I left Five Guys my life had been pure hell since then. I was now almost six months pregnant. I still hadn't told my mother or brother about it. I wanted to tell them, but I felt as if they were going to judge me. My mother and I didn't have a good relationship as it is. As far as my love life, it's in shambles. Calvin didn't want anything to do with me. Every time I called him, it would go straight to voicemail. I think he had me on block. I tried calling from my brother's phone, and he picked up the line, but as soon as he heard my voice, he would hang up immediately. The only thing I did was mope around the house. I only came out my room for school, to eat, shit, or shower. I was really under depression. I wouldn't eat unless I felt like it.

I started to get ready for school, which would be over soon. I couldn't wait till Marie and I got this plan over with. I hope she was still willing to do it with me. I hadn't talked to her since the day at Five Guys. It would be petty if I just hit her up before school talking about some damn set up. I really wanted to be a part of the dance team at MTSU, but by me being pregnant, it wouldn't be possible. I guess going through with this set up would be stupid as hell. I guess it wouldn't be right for me to ruin her life because I was being a jealous bitch. Shay was a great person, and I had no reason to be jealous of her. I think having this baby would change my attitude on certain things. I would just have to let my brother and mother know what was going on.

I smelled something cooking in the kitchen. It smelt like bacon, sausage, eggs, grits, and pancakes. This was my favorite breakfast meal. My mother would make this every morning when my father was alive. I missed my father so much. I'm upset that he wouldn't be able to witness the birth of my child. Walking in the kitchen, I saw my brother Chaz and mother sitting at the table talking. They both looked at me with disappointing faces. I began to get nervous wondering what was about to occur. I sat down at the end of the table to see what was going on. My stomach was in knots because my mother was crying.

"Mom, why are you crying?"

"Alexis, are you pregnant?"

"Um, maybe."

"You little whore. Who is the father?"

"Mom. Why are you calling me that? I'm keeping this baby. I will be a better mother to my child than you were to me."

"Listen here you little bitch. I did everything for you and Chaz. When your father died, he didn't leave me shit because of his family. They hate me because of my family. Your dad and I were not supposed to be together due to the beef with my family being the number one mafia family. "

"Well, I'm not the issue. You did not have to treat me that way because of them. I knew you hated the way dad treated me. He treated me like a princess, and you hated it. I got whatever I wanted, but you know what you don't have to be a part of me or my child life."

I got up from the table while the tears started falling. I couldn't believe my mother. I guess I would have to stay with my grandparents for a while. I couldn't understand why my mother hated me so much. I needed answers now. Once I got out of school today, I will be visiting my grandparents' house.

* * *

I FINISHED PICKING out my outfit for today. I decided on wearing my pink jumpsuit with some all-white Reeboks. I decided on wearing my hair in a messy bun. My stomach began to growl continuously, so before I headed off to school, I stopped at Chick-fil-A. That place was the best for breakfast. Sometimes I would stop by Waffle House, but it be too crowded in the morning before school. Everyone and they momma be trying to eat there. I glanced in the mirror to make sure I was presentable. My stomach was beginning to poke out a little bit. I rubbed my hands across my belly. Tears began to fall because I was amazed at how motherhood would be. I grabbed my backpack to leave out the house. I was stopped my mother embracing me with a hug. Rolling my eyes, I walked right past her. I wasn't about to give in to her apologies. My mother played victim all the time, and I wasn't for it today. Today was going to be a great day. Well, at least I was hoped so.

Pulling up to the school fifteen minutes later, I felt very nauseous and literally threw up everywhere. I needed a Canada Dry Ginger Ale to settle my stomach. I couldn't miss school today because graduation was some weeks away. I needed to get all my work done before my finals next week. I was barely passing all my classes due to me not coming to class on time. I regretted it, but I know I could get this work done. I wasn't a dumb girl, but I just hated doing homework. College was out the question for me right now. I didn't know what I wanted to do with my life. Since I was pregnant, I was going to wait college out for now. Looking at my phone, I received a notification on my phone from Instagram. It was from a familiar guy I used to talk about six months ago. He messaged me stating that he may be my baby's father. I couldn't remember even sleeping with him. I messaged him stating that I would meet him after school. I had too many things to worry about right now.

WALKING TOWARDS MY LOCKER, I noticed people were staring at me. I noticed a piece of paper on the floor with my Escort profile on there. I saw everyone laughing and pointing fingers at me. I heard some people saying I was a dirty hoe. Tears began to well up in my eyes. I knew Calvin had something to do with this. I know I did him wrong, but he didn't have to go this far. I would have never done this shit to him. I didn't even tell anyone about him being a two-minute nigga. He couldn't hold his nut longer enough for me to even get mine. I felt like shit at this moment. I began to feel dizzy and nauseated again. This had to be the lowest thing he could ever do to me. I wanted to get back at him, but I knew I had other things to handle.

Marie and Shay walked passed me with mugged looks on their faces. I didn't know what Marie's problem was. I thought we were supposed to be cool but apparently not. I still wanted my money from the nigga that I let her fuck for some money. Yes, Marie was a hoe as well. She just was undercover with hers. If Jerome found she trapped him with this pregnancy, he would want to dump her ass too. I wasn't into being petty, but he will find out one day.

I ignored everyone walking down the hallway. I went straight to my classroom to start on my work. I didn't have time for any drama or bullshit today. It was five minutes left before class, and I felt sick to my stomach. I saw these flyers on everyone's desk in class. I felt embarrassed and humiliated. Calvin was a true fuck boy for this. Now the whole school is going to know that I was a hoe. Tears began to well up when I saw my principal walk into my classroom speaking with my teacher. I put my head down to avoid any contact with anyone else. I couldn't be the laughing stock any more than I already was.

"Alexis Green, can you come with me please?" Principal Walker said while waiting for me at the door.

I gathered my things while everyone was staring at me taking pictures putting them on Snapchat. I knew someone probably had a meme going around already about me. I hated Calvin on my life right now. I was going to get revenge one way or another. The only reason he was doing this is because he wasn't good in the bedroom. I couldn't help he couldn't hold his nut. Hell, he was still young though, so maybe when he got older, he would get better. I guess love made you do crazy things. I knew he still loved me, but he couldn't admit it. He wanted attention, so he got it by embarrassing me. I just knew soon enough karma will come around.

Principal Walker and I had finally made it back to his office. I was scared shitless because my mother was sitting in there. Her face was so red, so I knew she was pissed off at me. I didn't know why I was here, but I knew it was bad. I didn't even try speaking to my mother. I just sat down and waited to see what I did.

"Ms. Green, do know why you are here?"

"No, if I knew then I would've come to you in asked you, right?"

"Well, it seems to me that you have skipped school way too many days to graduate with your class. You will have to graduate this summer. You will have to make up for all those days you didn't come. "

"Are you serious? Can I still go to prom?"

"No ma'am, you can't go to prom. You can't return to school until summer school starts."

"This some bullshit, man. Fuck this school, "I said while walking out of the office.

I walked out of school crying. I couldn't believe I wasn't going to be graduating with my other classmates. This was the worst thing I could've avoided, but I didn't. My life was completely over. I give up. There no need me to even be here. I just wanted to end my life at this very moment. I changed my mind when I felt my stomach move. My child had kicked for the first time. That's when I knew I had to change my life around because my child needed a role model.

SHAY

P rom Day

    Today was my senior prom. I was so excited about going to prom with Chauncey. I had so much shit to get done before tonight. I was now headed to the hair salon so that my stylist Will can slay this hair. I was going for the knot bun with a Chinese bang. My dress was a V-neck sequin court train sleeveless dress. It was all lavender with black trimmings. My girl Cheronda was going to hook my face up with the makeup. I couldn't wait to slay all these hoes tonight. I barely got dressed up because I was kind of a tomboy sometimes. I only wore tennis shoes. I was the girl that dressed casually all the time. Tonight, I planned on popping out on everyone who slept on me. I wanted them to remember this night and years after this night.

    My phone begins to ring, and I knew it was my love Chauncey. He was calling me back to back just to see if I was ready or not. I wasn't even half ready yet. I guess he just missed me. I had been working nonstop this week, and I didn't have a chance to see him. We both wouldn't see each other till later. The person that would be taking my pictures would be my girl, Arionna. She was cold with the pictures. I had known her since middle school. Supporting my friends was a big thing for me, so I wanted her to be a part of this special moment.

I arrived at the salon, noticing Alexis with some older man who was old enough to be her daddy. They were all cuddled up kissing and hugging. I am wondering why she was with old ass men. Was he her pimp, or was he the baby daddy? I had so many questions regarding this situation, but I was just going to mind my business. Walking towards the shop, I felt her staring a hole in my face. For her to have all that mouth, she was still scary as fuck. I was waiting for her ass to step to me.

"Hey Shay, you can't speak."

"Alexis, you know damn well I don't fuck with you that way. "

"Well bitch, what have I done to you?"

"You've always been against me since I got the spot of co-captain spot. I have never cared for you anyway. "

"Whatever, girl."

Walking into the salon, I needed to take a breath before I went off. I counted to ten to calm down a bit. I wasn't going to let her get me worked up over nothing. This was my prom day, and nobody will be stealing my joy. It was time for me to get slayed. Malachi was ready to wash my hair. Malachi was Marie's brother. He was the braider and shampoo tech at the shop. I wasn't really close with Malachi as I was with Marie. We were cordial, and that's it. See, Malachi was the messy gay type. He would stir up all this mess with folks and act he didn't do anything. I just kept him at a distance. I wasn't with the drama.

"Hey Shay, you ready for prom?"

"Yes, I'm very excited about it. Chauncey and I are gone be the power couple tonight."

"I know that's right. I'm not going to prom. I'm gay, and my boyfriend is not a people person. I'll just chill with him tonight. I hope you have a great night, love. "

"Thank you."

My head was feeling great now. Getting my hair washed was the reason I love coming to the salon. When someone washes it, it feels way better than me washing it myself. Malachi had just finished washing my hair when we heard someone arguing. We both ran out the washroom to see who it was. It was Alexis and this girl name Kita from the dance team. Kita was going off on her for being pregnant by her boyfriend. Alexis was on the floor crying and giving this big sob story on how it happened. Rolling my eyes, I walked over to the styling chair to get my hair braided. It was kind of funny that Alexis always slept with someone else's man when she had her own. Calvin was a great man to her. I hated she did him like that. I really hoped he would heal from this. He would be in my prayers.

Four Hours Later

I was headed back home to get ready for tonight. Thinking about my dress had me too geeked. My hair was slayed to the gods. My makeup blended so well with my skin tone. Cheronda did her thing on my face. I couldn't stop looking in the mirror at myself. I had posted so many pictures and videos on Snapchat already. I had gotten several compliments already. I couldn't stop feeling myself, so I bumped that Beyoncé song "Feeling Myself" until I got home.

Chauncey had sent me a freaky picture telling me to meet him at the spot. I agreed to it because I was horny now. I drove to the spot, and he was already parked. I smiled stepping out of the car. He was dressed in his red Jordan sweatpants, a black tank top, and some Nike flip-flops. His hair sported a fresh tapered fade with a part on the right of his head. He was looking so sexy standing next to his car. I grabbed his face while passionately kissing his lips. He twirled his tongue inside my mouth like a Twizzler. My panties began to get moist as he rubbed his fingers against my freshly shaved vagina. He placed two fingers inside, while I straddled his fingers. I began to pick up the pace as he got deeper and deeper trying to open me up. I picked up the pace, even more, feeling myself about to explode on his fingers with my juices. He whispered in my ear for me to get on top of the trunk. I looked at him like he was crazy. Chauncey was very spontaneous, and I liked every bit of it. He was bringing sides out of me that I didn't know about.

I hopped on top of the trunk and got on all fours. He then got behind me, while positioning me the way he wanted me. I arched my back and tooted my ass up so that he could just slide in. He began to slap his dick on my clit, teasing me just a bit, before slowly sliding his long chocolate pole inside this tight hole of mine inch by inch while matching my rhythm. He picked up his pace while grinding inside of me hitting my precious spot. I let out a soft moan letting him know I was enjoying this very moment. I felt myself about to explode again, so I started throwing this back harder so that he can cum with me. I loved the shit he would say while I threw it back.

"Shit, your pussy feels so good. Why you got to have so much power down there, girl?"

"Boy, shut up so that I can get this last nut."

He slid his big long pole back inside. I began to twerk on his dick so that he could go deeper inside me. Something about him being deep inside made me even wetter. He began to hit my g-spot harder. I couldn't contain myself, so here I was nutting for the third time. I was beginning to feel my hair sweating. I needed him to bust this nut so that I can go home, shower, and get ready. We would have more time to do this after prom. He began to pound my shit harder than usual. I knew when he did that he was about to bust a mean one. Minutes later, I felt his nut fill me up. Good thing I was on birth control. I reached into my purse grabbed my baby wipes to wipe myself off and wipe his dick off. We both kissed and headed home to get ready.

Ten minutes later, I saw all these cars surrounding my house. All my family members couldn't wait to see me off to prom. This is my last prom that I'm going to. It was so bittersweet. I began to tear up a bit, but I had to stop myself due to me having my makeup done. I was so ready to enjoy myself tonight. I was avoiding anything that would mess up my day. I prayed to God that there was no drama tonight at prom. I had a feeling that something was going to go wrong. I tried to think positive, but that intuition wasn't going away.

I noticed my mother car was there. I really wasn't trying to deal with her shit today. I just wanted to get ready and take pictures with my family. I walked in the door noticing my mother was arguing with my grandmother. She was telling my grandmother that she didn't appreciate her spending all that money on my prom. My mother was so selfish at times. I was the one paying for most of my stuff for prom. I didn't depend on nobody to do anything for me. I didn't want to hear anything about I owed someone some money. I didn't want those issues. I passed them both to avoid any other arguments.

"Damn bitch, you can't speak to your mother. "

"This is my prom day. I'm avoiding any negativity that tries to ruin my special day. "

"Well, I'm sorry. You look beautiful."

"Thank you."

I walked into my room to prepare myself for tonight. I had to take a quick shower to get the sex off of me. Hopping in the shower, I grabbed my Dove soap, lathering the soap against my body. I began to think about everything that had transpired throughout my high school years. Joining the dance team really boosted my self-esteem. I was struggling with confidence issues when I got to high school but being able to show my talent help to boost that ego. Hearing people give me compliments just made me feel great inside. I looked at the time realizing I had thirty minutes to get ready. I jumped out the shower and ran to my room to get ready. Good thing my dress was easy to put on.

"Grandma, come zip me up, please! "I yelled.

"Girl, don't be yelling at me. Turn around so I can zip you up."

"Granny, thank you for making this day so special for me."

"You're welcome, baby. I'm so proud of you. Remember to follow your heart and do what want to do in life. No matter what anyone else says, follow your dreams."

"I will, granny. I love you so much."

"I love you more."

We both headed to the living room. All my family was finally here to get pictures. I was about to have a whole photoshoot messing with them. Arionna had just arrived so that I wouldn't be getting tortured by my family anymore. Chauncey had texted me stating he was five minutes away. We were rolling in a red Range Rover tonight. His parents had the hookup. I couldn't wait to take pictures around it. I was going to slay with these pictures. I wanted everyone to know La'Shayla Barnes didn't come to play. I had finished up taking pictures with my family when I noticed my parents crying. I knew they were just crying happy tears, but they were both hugging each other. I didn't know what was up with that. Whatever it was, I prayed they were working on the issues.

Chauncey walked into the room in I stopped in my tracks. He was looking so handsome. I just wanted to take his ass to the back room and make love to him. He was rocking his black tuxedo with a lavender vest to match my dress. He had on some maroon sequined loafers to set off the outfit. We both looked amazing. He stared at me like I was the best thing he ever saw. I started blushing very hard. We both stood there for a couple of minutes just admiring each other's presence. His smile was intoxicating. He came closer to me while kissing me on the cheek. He blew his peppermint breath on my neck. It sent chills down my spine. I felt my panties get moist again, so I walked away from him to get more pictures with my family. Once the pictures were all taken, we were off to prom. I gave everyone hugs, kisses, and said my goodbyes. I didn't have a curfew tonight due to it being prom night. I was glad of that. I knew my parents would be calling every hour though. My Auntie Peaches gave some the gold pack Trojan condoms in case I needed them. I laughed because I didn't even use condoms with Chauncey.

On the drive to prom, I was so scared of Chauncey driving this Range Rover. He had road rage out the ass. I kept telling him to calm down, but he would laugh at me. He would just say he got it under control. I uploaded some pics of us on Snapchat and Instagram before heading into the Sheraton Hotel downtown. This was going to be a fun night, and hopefully, a memory I would never forget with the people I love.

MARIE

*H*ere it is prom day. I wasn't that excited about it because I would have to wear this fake baby bump. I was still faking this pregnancy. I just wanted to end this lie because it was getting out of hand. I would even lie to my granny and daddy about going to doctor appointments. Malachi knew I was hiding something, but he couldn't find out what it was. He would always bust through my room trying to be nosy. I wasn't going to get my hair fancy today. I was going to my girl Destiny for some lemonade braids. I wanted them very long like Nikki Minaj in that "MotorSport" video. I didn't want to wear a weave like everyone else I wanted to be different. I was wearing a pink tulle sleeveless mermaid dress with glitter pumps to match. I wasn't going to wear much makeup due to the fact my skin was very sensitive. I just wanted to stay as natural as possible.

Headed to get my hair braided, I got a call from Jerome but didn't answer it. Jerome was still begging me to take him back after that incident some weeks ago. I forgave him, but he put his hands on me. I just couldn't get over that. I know he was supposed to be my date, but I wanted to go by myself. I didn't have time to deal with his ass today. I put him on do not disturb so that he wouldn't be able to contact me while I was getting ready for tonight. My granny and father were renting me an all-black Camaro for the weekend. I was so excited because that was my dream car. I wanted one as a graduation gift, but I knew it would be impossible for them to get. I just prayed I had enough money saved up to purchase it. I couldn't wait till my homeboy David took my pictures later in it. He wasn't even going to charge me for the picture, which was a plus. Tonight was going to be lit. I couldn't wait to sit on these hoes neck tonight with this dress and hairstyle.

I arrived at Destiny house twenty minutes later. Thank God, I washed my hair before I got here because it wouldn't take her that long to braid it. I notice a familiar car that was parked in the driveway. I just couldn't think of who car it was. I walked in the house noticing Chaz and Destiny were having a deep conversation. They were having a conversation about Alexis. I hid in the corner to see what the conversation was about. I knew it would be juicy. I heard Chaz state that Alexis was pregnant by one of our teachers at school. I wondered who it was. We had some fine ass teachers there, so I was a bit confused. Alexis had a way of flirting with people so it could've anyone. Then I heard him say something about Mr. Alex Adkins. I knew she was fucking off with him when I caught Alexis coming out of his room with her shirt undone. She was lying to me this whole time. I couldn't believe that bitch. Mr. Adkins had a wife and two kids. Here she was being a side bitch to a nigga that didn't really want her ass, and he was just using her for sex.

I came from behind the corner shocking them both. They both looked at me like they seen a ghost. I knew Destiny remembered she had to do my hair today. I saw her motioning me to sit in the chair. Chaz was looking fine as hell standing there by the wall. He was tatted all over his body. I loved a man who was tatted everywhere on his body. He had a tattoo over his left eye that said mafia. I wonder why he had that tatted. In the back of my head, I had so many questions. He had golds on the top front row of his teeth. I could tell he was mixed with something. I didn't know why Alexis was hiding her fine ass brother from me. That was very selfish of her. Chaz was very attractive. I wondered if he was talking to anyone now. I would love to get a taste of him. I decided to get up and walk to the bathroom to get his attention while I walked by. I knew he would be looking at my ass since I had on this short blue jean romper. I turned around, and he was smiling from ear to ear.

"You like what you see huh?"

"What makes you think that?"

"It's the way you are looking me when I walk past you."

"I might just want to get to know you better. Is that a problem with you?"

"No, it was never a problem, boo."

"Well, here let me put my number in your phone. Hit me up anytime you need me, Ms. Who?"

"My name is Marie. Your name is?"

"I'm Chaz. I'll see you around. Don't be a stranger. "

When he walked out that door, I couldn't keep my eyes off him. That boy was fine as hell. If only my black ass weren't still stuck on Jerome, I would fuck him. I hope he didn't have female issues because he would be my man one day. I saw Destiny coming from the back room and sat back down to get my hair braided. She smelled like a whole loud pack of weed. I didn't even know she smoked weed. It was always the pretty girls smoking weed. I wonder if her boyfriend was the one who influenced her to do that. I didn't say anything I just kept my mouth closed. I sat there quietly until she finished my hair. I didn't want to start a conversation up because my head was banging. Destiny was so damn heavy handed. I popped like three Advil gel cap to relieve some of the pain.

* * *

AN HOUR or so later Destiny was finally done with my hair. I glanced in the mirror to see the results of my hair. She had done her thang on my hair. I was impressed on how she put the designs in my braids. Destiny really had a gift. I hoped that one day she was able to get her own braiding shop. I always let her do my hair. My hair was so healthy due to her doing it every two or three weeks. I only stayed loyal to one person who put up with this mess on this head of mine. I gave her money for doing my hair, booked my next appointment, and headed to the nail shop. My girl Trang was going to hook my nails up. I was going to get the coffin shape nails. I wanted to get my nails plain and simple. I may add some type of design since it was my prom day. I knew my girl could freestyle if she needed to. Her nail work was cold. I just hope they weren't booked today since I didn't make an appointment.

Ten minutes later, I was in the chair getting my feet done. Trang was doing someone else's nails. I noticed it was Alexis in the chair. She was just the person I wanted to see. I was kind of surprised that she didn't even look my way. I saw her stomach had a bigger pudge to it. I just turned the other way. I was glad she left before I did. The drama I wasn't trying to deal with it.

Arriving back home thirty minutes, I needed to take a shower before putting on my dress. I noticed Jerome car was parked outside. I just know he didn't show up to my house without letting me know. I walked in the house, and he was on the couch dressed up with his prom shit on. I don't know why he was here like he was taking me to prom. I didn't want to go with him. I walked straight past his ass like he wasn't even there. I sensed his eyes gazing at me while I strolled to my room. I couldn't entertain him at that second. I was ready to get my dress on. David would be here to take pictures in thirty minutes.

"Granny!" I yelled.

"Marie, chile, why are you yelling in this house? You know I don't allow that in this house."

"Granny, I need help fixing my dress. Can you zip me up, please?"

"Yes baby, you look amazing sweetie. I have a surprise for you. "

"What is it, granny?"

"Come in the living room."

Walking in my room, I saw the person I wanted to see— my mother. Tears began to well up in my eyes. Malachi had walked in the door instantly with tears in his eyes. We both hugged our mother. She looked the same. I could tell she was aging because of the gray streaks in her hair. We hugged for like another minute and went to take pictures before I left. I decided to change my mind about going to prom with Jerome. I didn't want my parents finding out about him hitting me, so I just went. I made sure he understood this as well. He would get confused if I didn't acknowledge what this was. After taking pictures, we headed off to prom. With a great night headed towards us, I was so excited. I just hoped that tonight ended with no drama.

We both arrived at the Sheraton Hotel downtown. I didn't have anything to say to Jerome. I had to give him props though; he was being a gentleman. He was opening doors, holding my hand, and kissing my forehead. I saw Shay and Jerome walking into the door as well. I knew she wasn't going to be upset about me being with Jerome. I couldn't worry about what she thought. I was here to enjoy my night. Other people opinions didn't matter at this point. I walked with my head held high with a smile on my face.

"Hey, Marie."

"Hey girl, you look beautiful."

"Thank you, so do you. Enjoy your night."

"You as well."

Walking off to the room where prom was, I noticed Alexis walking in. I saw her holding hands with Mr. Adkins. Everyone stopped what they were doing. She was bold as hell walking in this place knowing he had a wife at home. I suddenly lost all respect for her. That was so disrespectful of her. Alexis thought that shit was cute, but it wasn't all. I walked up to her so that I can confront her ass. I was not about to let this go down tonight.

"Alexis."

"What, girl?"

"Why are you doing this? Everyone knows you slept with Mr. Adkins. This man is married with children."

"Look who wants to bring up children. Tell Jerome how you aborted the child you claim you pregnant with. Tell everyone how you didn't want the baby because you were scared. Tell that shit."

"Girl, whatever. I don't have time for this shit. Tell everyone how you got expelled from school and you will not be walking across that stage. "

Alexis walked off humiliated. I knew she felt some type of way after I said that. I also felt bad. Now everyone knew my secret about aborting my child. This wasn't the first time I aborted a child though. I had killed both of my children. I just couldn't be a teen mom. I saw Jerome glancing at me with a smug on his face. I strolled down the hall to explain to him the reason behind this.

"Jerome, WAIT!"

"Marie, wait for what. I almost gave my life up for you. I can't even believe this shit. You killed a child due to your selfish ways. I was going to take care of my child. Thank God, I dodge that bullet. I don't need you. I never did. It's over, Marie. See you around."

Jerome walked off. Tears began to well up in my eyes. I couldn't blame anyone but myself. I felt bad for trying to ruin his life by faking this pregnancy the whole time. I lost my boyfriend and probably my best friend on my prom night. My grandmother always told me never to lie because it would lead to a bigger problem. I wish I would've listened. I was more hurt now than anyone else. What a great way to start my prom night off!!!

JEROME

The night of prom I had gotten the answer I needed. Marie was not pregnant. Her ass was faking the whole damn time. I'm so thankful that I didn't let go of my basketball scholarship for her selfish ass. I was kind of glad she got the abortion because I didn't want the child anyway. I wasn't ready for a baby. I wanted to play basketball and make it to the pros one day. The night after prom, I dropped Marie off and headed home. We didn't do anything but go to Waffle House with the other classmates. Marie wasn't talkative due to the fact everyone knew what she did. I wasn't gone judge her or anything because I couldn't. I just hated the fact she lied to me with a straight face. The tension between her and Shay was thick. I knew Shay didn't agree with her talking to me after I hit her. That was just a mistake though. I learned my lesson about putting my hands-on women. I knew that it wasn't right to take my anger out with my fist.

I was glad to be taking some anger management classes. The classes were really helping me with my anger. I would've invited Marie, but I knew she would've rejected the offer. I missed her at times, but that relationship was over with. I was trying to focus on school in the fall. I was going to school to be a sports personal trainer. I loved sports, so I wanted to get a degree in something I would use in the future. I would be graduating with honors and a 3.5 grade point average. I know it seemed like I was bullshitting, but when it came to schoolwork, I made sure I stayed focused. I was glad Marie dropped those charges on me. I wasn't trying to go to court and do community service for that bullshit. I promised myself that I wouldn't put my hands on anyone in the future. That was a wakeup call for me. I wanted to follow the plan God had for me.

Later today, I will be going to MTSU to get signed up for the fall semester. I will be staying on campus to get away from my family. For me to become more independent, I wanted to stay in a dorm. Even though my mother was scared shitless about me staying on campus, I had a long talk with her on why I chose to do that. I just wanted to be away from Braxton with all his drug dealing business. I didn't want to be at the house when he got busted for selling drugs out my mother's house. Both my parents were going with me to help me with any paperwork. My parents were back on talking terms now. My dad came over more to spend time with my mom. I could see my mother getting her glow back from a couple of months ago. I don't know what they had going on, but I was sure going to ask. It would be great if they worked on the marriage though. They both had been married for too long to end now.

* * *

Two days later

It was finally graduation day. I was excited but nervous at the same time. After today, I would have my whole life ahead of me. It was up to me if I would be successful. I was going to school and staying focused on my schoolwork. I didn't want to get distracted by anything. I can't believe four years of high school had already passed. It felt like I had just started high school. Graduation would be at six o'clock this evening, but we had practice this morning. I hated this getting up early crap. I was not a morning person at all. I just dealt with it since I had to get up for school and practice.

Headed to graduation practice, I couldn't get Marie off my mind. It was like I would think of her day and night. I guess I just needed closure that I ended the relationship with her. I just wanted to make sure she was alright. I know she would be at practice this morning. I would just try to have a conversation with her avoiding any drama. She had a very nasty attitude at times, so I wanted to avoid that. Regardless of anything that happened, I wanted to remain friends. Life was too short, and I didn't want to stay on bad terms due to our break up.

I arrived at the Municipal Auditorium. I saw my boys Calvin and Chauncey standing outside smoking a blunt. Those niggas were bold as hell doing that, knowing there were police everywhere in that area. I would've hit the blunt, but I know my coach has random drug tests. I wasn't trying to get caught up doing that shit so close to the end. By looking their eyes, they were lit as fuck. I grabbed my eye drops so that they could drop them in before practice. I didn't want them getting caught and sent home on our special day.

"What's up, bros?"

"Nothing man, ready to get this practice over so that we can go eat. We got the munchies."

"Y'all niggas stay high. I don't see how y'all do it. What y'all got planned after graduation?"

"Well, Chauncey, Braxton, and me are hitting up Atlanta. Braxton wants to ride with him to make a sell. Plus, we may hit up the strip club as well. I need a damn break from Nashville."

"Y'all need to be careful hanging with Braxton. That nigga is trouble seriously. I would ride with y'all, but I ain't trying to get caught up in some shit."

"Man, just come with us. We gone able to get lit and celebrate our graduation. Plus, you single now.

"Alright man. I'll let my people know. "

I really wasn't up to going to this trip with my niggas, but I did need a break from Nashville for a bit. I knew my parents wouldn't trip about me going because Braxton would be there as well. I was just iffy about it though. Braxton was going to make a deal with these mafia people. I know Chaz and Alexis was connected to them. I eavesdropped on Braxton talking to someone about meeting them in Atlanta for a drug deal. I knew this would be a dangerous thing to do. The mafia family didn't play when it came to their money. Word on the street was that Braxton owed them almost over $10, 000 dollars. I guess Braxton had been using their product and selling it at a cheaper price, or they probably could be after our family. I had no idea what was going on. I just prayed things didn't get ugly.

Walking into the auditorium, I noticed Marie talking to Shay. I guess they had got over their issues. It was a good feeling seeing them talking again. They both had a close bond and strong friendship. I walked towards them to say hello. I knew Shay would probably have an attitude. I just wanted to apologize. I wanted to right all my wrongs before we all crossed the stage that night. They both were looking beautiful standing there all natural— no makeup, with messy hair buns, with their matching Victoria Secret jogging suits on. I saw Chauncey walk up to Shay giving her a passionate kiss. I wish I could've done the same to Marie, but I knew it would give her mixed feelings.

"Hey, ladies, I just want to apologize for my actions lately."

"We accept your apology. "

"Everyone, please find your name on the seat and sit down, please. We are trying to get done as quickly as possible!" Ms. Adams shouted over the microphone.

We all went to find our seats to be seated. I wasn't close to no one that I was cool with. I kept looking over at Marie. She was even more beautiful just sitting there waiting on her name to be called. I will catch her staring at me as well. I knew we both missed each other, but it was time to go our separate ways. Our practice was going great until Alexis showed, causing a scene. She had the nerve to come here knowing she wasn't walking across the stage. Then she exposed Mr. Adkins eating her pussy in the classroom at school. After, prom, Mr. Adkins had broken it off with her. She was in her feelings still, and she made herself look bad.

GRADUATION

Hear it was the time of my life I've been waiting for to walk across this stage. I was proud to be graduating with honors with my homies Calvin and Chauncey. Through the good and bad days, we pushed through. I was glad to have some true friends during the four years I was here. They both were there when I needed to vent or just have a wonderful time. I began to get teary-eyed seeing my parents and other family members cheering me on. I was almost close to walking this stage.

"Jerome Hamilton."

They called my name, and I felt so pleased after I grabbed my diploma and ran off the stage. I crossed that finish line. I started juggin' to my seat. I saw people cheering me and laughing. I looked up at my parents and said thank you. I couldn't have done without their support and guidance. My mom was shedding so many tears. She was so damn sensitive at times. I sat down and waited for everyone else to cross the stage. After everyone's name was called, we threw our hats up and chanted class of 2010. We all walked out to find our families. I saw Marie walking by herself. I just wanted to kiss her sweet lips.

"Hello, Marie."

"Hello, Jerome."

"What you are doing tonight?"

"I don't have any plans. I'm going home since I must work tomorrow. What are you doing?"

"The boys and I going to Atlanta in the morning. My brother has to handle some business."

"Please be careful, Jerome. I heard that it was a setup. Chaz and Alexis are trying to set him up. I just wanted to let you know. "

"Thank you."

After Marie had given me that information, I was scared shitless. I didn't want my brother or any of my friends getting hurt. I needed to inform my brother about this shit. I wasn't about to let him go down like that. Even though I didn't approve of the things he did, family will always be first, and I had his back regardless.

CHAUNCEY

I know everyone is in love with me at this point. Yes, I'm a true gentleman. I believe in being faithful to my girlfriend. I don't like having several girls. Having one girl is enough for me. See, Shay was the girl that I always wanted. I was crushing on her all these years of high school, but I waited until senior because I suffered from low self-esteem. I had some big ass teeth, which made it so I could barely keep my mouth closed. People were very cruel and picked on me all the time. It wasn't until I got braces that things got a little better. I begged my parents to allow me to get them. I just wanted to boost my ego. Once I got them on, I felt like a whole new person.

I'm Chauncey Lavon Jones. I'm the oldest of three children. I have a brother Charles Jones who is sixteen, and my sister Charity who is fourteen. See, we weren't from the United States. My father and mother were both from Somalia. My parents were very wealthy and owned several businesses here in Nashville. My mom owned a flower shop and a hair salon. My dad owned several vending machines and corner stores. Even though they had money, I still worked my ass off to get what I wanted. I also sold weed on the side as well. I kept that a secret from everyone because I knew my people would trip. I would just sell the weed out my car outside of the house. I know that was a dangerous thing to do, but I had to make my money some type of way.

I would get my product from my nigga Braxton. He was the nigga whose shit would get you lit as fuck. He told me that he got his shit from California. My shit always sold quickly because I always had clientele. Most of my homies smoked weed, so it was a good look on my end. Braxton fucked with me real tough. I know his best friend Chaz was feeling some type of way. He was a true crybaby ass bitch. He had been bitching about Braxton not fronting him more product like he was giving me. I didn't like that nigga at all. I felt like he was jealous of Braxton. He would always say slick shit. Braxton would laugh shit off, but I didn't like it. It has been times where I wanted to confront him, but I left it alone.

ATLANTA TRIP

Today was the day Braxton, Calvin, Jerome, and Chaz would be going to Atlanta. It wasn't really supposed to be a business trip. We were supposed to be celebrating our graduation. Chaz wasn't even supposed to be going with us. I think he was something fishy. He had mentioned to Braxton that he couldn't come because he had to work. But early this morning as we were leaving, he called him saying he was going. I told Braxton I didn't have a good feeling about this so-called sell he had. I was wondering why they couldn't come to Nashville to give him the product. My intuition kept saying it was a setup. I prayed to God nothing happened down here.

"Braxton."

"Yea, bro?"

"You sure about this man? I have a feeling this is a setup. Chaz is up to something I know it."

"Just chill, bro. Everything is cool. I got this under control."

"Alright. I sure hope you got it under control.

In the car, Shay was texting me. I was trying to get me some rest, but she was irritating me. I know she's worried, but she needed to stay calm. I told her I would text her once I get there. I was grateful for her though. I could tell she really cared about me, but I needed some space at times. I know she was upset at me. Her lil attitude was cute, especially when she pouted. Whenever she didn't get her way, she would pout and get mad. That just meant she wanted some of this long chocolate piece of meat. I would give her that raw, passionate sex and take her out to eat. That would always solve the issue. I guess I'll Cash App her some money so that she could spend some bands. I was falling for her ass super tough. No matter what, we will always be straight.

* * *

We finally had arrived in Atlanta. They decided to head to Lenox Mall. I wasn't in the mood to be shopping. I just wanted to find somewhere to eat and chill. I saw Chaz catching an Uber to go somewhere. I wonder where this nigga was going. I knew something fishy was going on. It was time I confront his fake ass. Why didn't he ask anyone else to go with him? Nigga thought he was slick, but I was watching his every move. I thought about catching an Uber to follow him. I just needed to see where he was going. He was really showing how true of a snake he was. I told the homies I'll be right back. I lied and told them that I was getting a surprise for Shay.

The Uber arrived within the next five minutes. It was cool but dangerous at the same time. I told the man driving the car to follow the other car ahead. We drove for like an hour to Savannah, Georgia. This city looked country as hell. *Who the hell was he meeting here?* We finally got to the stop. It was this big ass house. It was a mansion. I watched as he went towards the house. I got out the car to follow him.

"Wait right here."

Walking away from the Uber driver I gave him some extra cash for the waiting. I saw this man that looked exactly like Chaz. I wonder if that was the man who was so-called dead. I tried to get a lil closer so that I could hear what they were saying. His dad was stating that Chaz needed to get Braxton to the house tonight. I heard them talking about getting revenge. Apparently, Braxton's dad got killed from using the drugs Julio was providing to him. He died from an overdose of the drugs. They were beefing because he was using the product instead of selling it. Braxton wasn't even his dad son. Braxton was Julio's son. Braxton's mother came out the house looking so beautiful. Chaz was pissed to see his dad with Braxton's mom. I guess that was his true love. She had gotten treatment and was living the best life she could. I had to text Braxton to let him know where the location was. Braxton needed to know this news. I couldn't keep this from him. I needed to keep my mouth shut.

Walking back toward the Uber, Shay began to call. I ignored her call due to the shit that was going on. I didn't need her panicking. It was beginning to get dark outside. Braxton was on his way due to the fact Chaz texted him saying he was in danger. Since they were tight, he was going to be there for his friend. They will no longer be friends after today. I decided to take a nap before they got here.

Me: Hey bae, I'm about to take a nap. Call you later.

Shay: I'm worried about you. Please call when you wake up, babe. I love you.

Me: I love you too, babe.

I instantly dozed off. I was tired as shit. It seems like these past few days I haven't gotten much rest. I said a small pray before I went to sleep.

I WOKE when I heard someone arguing outside of the car. It was Jerome and Braxton about doing this sell. Jerome had a funny feeling just like I did. I saw Calvin trying to come in between them. Braxton was stupid and stubborn. I decided to hop out the Uber to let him know what was up. As soon as I hopped out the car, I saw Chaz walking out the house. Then I saw Braxton's mother come out. I knew it was about to be some shit. They both walked towards everyone.

"Hey son, I heard you were putting friends over your blood brother."

"Ma, what the fuck are you talking about blood?"

"So, your auntie didn't tell you that Julio is your daddy?"

"How the hell is he my father? I was told my father died due to a drug overdose, or he died in a drug deal gone bad. Now what is true and what is not true?"

"Son, your dad is Julio the other man that died was some nigga I fooled around with when Chaz mother was with Julio. I had sex with both at the same time. Didn't know who your father was until the paternity test came back. "

"This some straight bullshit bruh. My whole life has been a fucking lie."

"Just calm down, son. So was is this I hear you letting this Chauncey boy get more product than Chaz. You need to let your brother be the one getting the product. "

"Man, fuck all that. Fuck him too."

Braxton began to walk back to the car so that he could make this sell. Chaz ran behind him like a little bitch. I began to walk towards the car as well. I needed to make sure Chaz didn't try anything stupid. Chaz must've felt me walking towards them and turned around.

"Nigga, what the hell you want? We don't need you following us."

"This a free damn country nigga. I can walk where I want to, snake ass bitch."

"Nigga, I'll never be a snake. You're a follower nigga, following Braxton around like a puppy."

"Nigga, you jealous, ain't ya? You mad I get more clientele than you. Maybe if you weren't fucking your brother's baby mama, maybe you would have more people to sell to. "

I heard gunshots going off. I saw Julio and his crew shooting everywhere. I saw Alexis with tape around her tied up. I wonder what the fuck was going on. Was Alexis trying to go against her family? This was some crazy shit. I heard more gunshots going off. Before I could run, something pierced my rib. I fell to the ground instantly. I grabbed my rib noticing the blood oozing out. I began to get light-headed. I grabbed my phone to call Shay. I had to tell her I loved her before I left this earth.

"Hey baby, I've been shot. I love you. Goodbye."

TO BE CONTINUED

KEEP READING FOR A SNEAK PEEK
OF GUILTY PLEASURES 2: A LOVE
TRIANGLE

MARIE

DAMN!!! I looked over in my passenger seat in noticed that my work clothes weren't there. *How could I forget?* I gripped the steering wheel, pressed the gas, and sped back home.

I noticed Jerome was at the crib. Shay was nowhere to be found. This would be a great opportunity to pursue him. An evil grin plastered across my face. This was the day that will change both of our lives.

In high school, Jerome was my crush. I envied Shay because she had taken him away from me. It was crazy because she knew he was my boyfriend. Jerome was the one that was supposed to be in love with me not her. Shay had betrayed our friendship, and she would never be forgiven for it.

I walked in the house noticing Jerome was watching television. Admiring him from afar just gave my body a tingling sensation. If only Jerome could make my world complete. I walked to my room to dress in something more appealing. I had to work in an hour, but I had other plans on my mind. I quickly texted my manager to let her know my car was having issues. I was not going to work today.

I changed into my lingerie, which was purchased from Vickie

Secrets two weeks ago. I sprayed some of my Moonlight perfume on, checked myself in the mirror, put some lip gloss on, and headed towards the living room.

Walking into the living room, I playfully grabbed the remote out of his hand.

"Damn Marie, I was watching that."

"Well, I'm sorry baby," I said while getting on top of him.

"Marie, what are you doing?"

"What you mean? Jerome, you know you want me. I'm the one you really supposed to be with. You just had to go get with my best friend. That really hurt my heart. I just want to be yours. Can I be yours, Jerome, please?" I begged him.

I began to straddle him. I could feel his bulge rising inside his pants.

"Marie we can't do this. It isn't right."

"Jerome, shut up nigga." Your dick is telling me otherwise. Don't act like you don't want me. I see the way you stare at me when Shay isn't looking."

I got up to remove the lingerie that I was wearing. His eyes begin to roam from my breasts down to my feet. I could tell he wanted to fuck the shit out of me. Dropping to my knees, he placed his nine inches in my mouth. I grabbed the Starburst from the table, placing it inside my mouth. I began to suck his dick in a slow motion until I got comfortable. Having the Starburst in my mouth made his dick taste even better. I glanced at him noticing he was enjoying every moment of it.

"Just like that," Jerome moaned.

Jerome placed his hand on the back of my head. I watched as his head dropped back. I picked up the pace while keeping my eyes on him. I got up to kiss him and massaged his shaft.

"I want some dick, Jerome."

Jerome stood up with his dick in his hand and watched me very carefully. Jerome was very fascinated by my body, but when he saw my juices dripping from my womanhood, his dick grew even more.

Jerome's thick long pole grew about three inches longer as he stepped out of his boxers, and he slowly stroked himself as I got completely naked. I saw the veins in his penis very clearly, and he was ready for this love session of ours.

"Do you have a condom?"

"Naw nigga, I'm on the pill. We will be fine, baby."

I lied, knowing damn well I wasn't on the pill. I didn't want to use a condom. I wanted my plan to work for the better. Jerome will regret everything he ever did to me. I wanted revenge, and I was going to do whatever I can to get it. I just hope my plan worked out because I didn't need anybody coming in between that.

Jerome turned me around so that I could face the television. I held on the living room table while he entered me from behind. It had been so long since I felt a man's dick inside me. I was so tight that he could barely get it in. So, he got down in ate my pussy from behind. He licked and slurped on my pussy so good that I instantly came in his mouth. Jerome finally got back up and rammed his dick into me fast.

"Damn, Jerome, don't be so rough baby."

"Shut the hell up, Marie. I ain't tryna make love. Just take this dick.
"

He began to take control pounding his dick and out of me. I let out a loud moan while throwing my ass back on him. My rhythm began to match as we both were trying to reach our nut. Inch by inch he got deeper inside of me. My legs began to weaken by the minute. I don't know how long I was going to be to take this standing up. I gripped Jerome's dick tighter as I began to throw it back hard and fast. My juices were flowing all over his big dick.

"Yes, daddy, go deeper! Please go deeper!

"You like that shit, don't you?"

"Yesss, I do!"

Jerome pulled me by my waist so that he could go even deeper inside me. I couldn't take this shit even more. My legs were trembling so bad as I began to reach my climax.

"Jerome, I'm about to …

He continued to fuck me so hard I could barely scream. I knew the next-door neighbors were enjoying every moment of this. Jerome gripped my waist so tight that my pussy began to grip his dick even tighter. Minutes later, he filled all his seeds inside of me.

CPSIA information can be obtained
at www.ICGtesting.com
Printed in the USA
LVOW10s2131170518
577556LV00012B/1011/P